RED HOT

A TABOO TREAT

WINTER

Mandy,
This redhead bites back!
♡ KWebster

K WEBSTER

August is bitter and cold.
Two people he loved most betrayed him.

Winter is hot and sultry.
She's the enemy's daughter.

A blowout fight between Winter and her dad
sends her straight into August's waiting arms.
But August doesn't want to hold her…he
wants revenge.

The two are an explosive combination
whenever they're together. August
antagonizes and Winter pushes back. Under
all the hate burning between them is an
attraction so intense, neither can ignore it.

It's only a matter of time before it consumes
them both.

A SHORTENED VERSION OF THIS BOOK IS
CURRENTLY AVAILABLE IN AUDIO ON THE
READ ME ROMANCE PODCAST.

Listen for FREE here:

iTunes: http://geni.us/A888vRA
Google Play: http://geni.us/7lB4UBK
Website: www.readmeromance.com

K WEBSTER'S TABOO WORLD

Welcome to my taboo world! These stories began as an effort to satisfy the taboo cravings in my reader group. The two stories in the duet, *Bad Bad Bad*, were written off the cuff and on the fly for my group. Since everyone seemed to love the stories so much, I expanded the characters and the world. I've been adding new stories ever since. Each book stands alone from the others and doesn't need to be read in any particular order. I hope you enjoy the naughty characters in this town! These are quick reads sure to satisfy your craving for instalove, smokin' hot sex, and happily ever afters!

Bad Bad Bad

Coach Long

Ex-Rated Attraction

Mr. Blakely

Malfeasance

Easton

Crybaby

Lawn Boys

Renner's Rules

The Glue

Dane

Enzo

Red Hot Winter

Several more titles to be released soon!

Thanks for reading!
K

DEDICATION

To my husband—the dirty inspiration behind
every taboo treat.

RED HOT WINTER

A TABOO TREAT

ONE

August

My daughter Callie chatters on the other end of the line, praising me for being such a good father. For always doing the right thing. Guilt niggles inside me, but I quickly ignore it. There's no room in my world for guilt.

Aside from my daughter, the only thing I have room for is hate and fury bubbling up inside me. My ex-wife, Jackie, Callie's mother, is responsible for my rage. She lit the match and tossed it in the gasoline when she decided to not only shack up with my best friend Tony, but to then marry him too. It's been two years since our bitter divorce and I still get pissed as fuck whenever I think about it.

"She'll be there after school," she says, dragging me from my angry thoughts. "I have cheer practice and then I'm going to dinner with

Landon, Lauren, and their dad. Do you think you can handle it okay?"

I reach over and grab my tumbler full of whiskey as I stare out the giant windows of my sleek, modern condo that overlooks downtown. It's the first day of December and it's snowing. I hate the damn snow. I hate the holidays. I hate fucking everything. "I can handle her fine."

Back when Tony and I were friends, I thought his daughter Winter was a cool kid. She loved my daughter like a sister and didn't cause too much trouble. The girl wasn't on my radar. When the divorce went down, I avoided any and all situations that involved Tony so I didn't accidentally ram my fist through his nose. But now? Now, Callie says Winter is in trouble at home and needs a place to stay. At first, I'd been adamant about telling my daughter no. Then, the more I thought about it, the more a plan developed.

I'll piss her off. Rile her up. Tell her what a piece of shit her dad is. Send her back to them with her tail between her legs. It makes me a dick, but I don't care. They fucking deserve it.

"Dad?"

I sip my drink and then smile. "I said I can handle her fine."

"I want you to try to be nice, though," she says softly. "I know things are strained with you and her dad, but please don't take it out on her."

"I would never," I say through clenched teeth. Lies. I'm dying to taunt and terrorize her. Just because I can.

"You're a terrible liar," she responds, amusement in her voice. "Luckily, she can handle her own. I'll call tomorrow to see how it went. Thanks, Dad. I love you."

"Love you too, kid."

We hang up and I drain the rest of my whiskey. I came home early from the office for this shit. Once I rise from my white leather chair, I inspect my space with scrutiny. This new condo I was forced to buy after the divorce is perfect for a bachelor like myself. My wife got the house, kept the kid, and moved that motherfucker into my bed. I could have fought for it considering she was the unfaithful one, but there was no way I could stomach being in that house ever again.

So I gave it up and got this two-bedroom condo that cost twice as much as my old house. I went through a bit of a phase where I bought whatever the fuck I wanted because I could. Because I deserved it for enduring what Jackie had put me through. My car is ridiculously overpriced, but I love it. At forty-one, I'm going through some midlife crisis bullshit that was set into motion because of Jackie's whorish ways.

I crack my neck and stalk through the house. Everything is white and clean. Not a pillow moved out of place. The door to Callie's room when she comes stays closed because she's a bit of a mess maker. I let her do her thing behind the door, but the rest of the condo remains immaculate.

The doorbell rings and a sliver of anticipation courses through me. Most men would take issue with terrorizing a sweet, innocent little eighteen-year-old girl. I'm not most men. I'm going to enjoy every second of it.

When I swing the door open, all the anticipation deflates like a balloon. A woman with dark bottle-dyed red hair in a black beanie has her head tilted down as she rummages around in her purse. Her shirt is low-cut and her perky tits are on full display despite the fact it's snowing outside. The black leather jacket she's wearing is tight and stylish, but I don't understand how it keeps her warm from the cold. She wears a pair of skinny jeans and some UGGs just like Callie made me buy her a few weeks ago.

I try to flip through all the Tinder dates I've had over the past few months to see if she's been one of them. Certainly not my type or anyone I'd willingly choose. I might have swiped right for her tits, though. Did we fuck? Is she back for round two? Disgust ripples through me. I wasn't this man before my divorce. I was fucking happy and loyal. Now, I just drift from woman to woman, unable to let go of my anger long enough to let one get close to me. I fuck and run. They never get a round two.

"Sorry, lady, but I'm going to have to pass," I grunt out and start to close the door.

Her head jerks up and big brown eyes bore into me. Familiar brown eyes. *His* brown eyes.

"Winter?" Last I remember, she had fucking braces and brown hair. She didn't look so… fuckable.

"Mr. Miller," she greets with a forced smile and then it's gone. "Thanks for letting me crash." She starts forward and I block the doorway. Her eyes narrow as she tilts her head up to look at me. My nostrils flare as I inhale the scent of cinnamon.

"I have rules." My voice is cold despite the way blood rushes to my dick. "Rules that little girls like you have to abide by."

Her brow arches up in challenge and her brown

eyes burn with intensity. "Let's hear them then."

Clenching my jaw, I take a step back to put some distance between us and cross my arms over my chest. My gaze falls to her tits.

"For one, you can't wear that shit in my house."

She laughs and it sounds sweet almost. Angelic even. That is until she cuts it off and glowers at me. "I'll wear whatever I want."

Smirking, I shrug. "Suit yourself. You'll get the side eye from every rich bitch in this complex."

Her cheeks redden slightly, her only tell of her embarrassment, before she challenges me with another hard glare. "And why is that?"

"Because this"—I wave at her outfit—"doesn't belong here."

She rolls her eyes. "Callie warned me you were a dick these days. I can handle myself with judgmental women. I do it all the time with your wife."

"Ex," I snap.

Her laugh is mocking. "Whatever. She's a bitch too." She pushes past me, dragging a suitcase in behind her.

Last I remember of this girl, she was a little teenager. Not this…woman. My eyes track her ass as she waltzes through my condo like she owns the goddamn place. Her jeans are tight and hug the round globes of her curvy ass, making my mouth water at the sight. For a brief second, I forget she's my daughter's friend—the daughter of the man I hate—and admire her for what she is.

Red. Hot. Female.

My cock is aching and straining against my suit slacks, desperate to pin her against the wall. But I can't fucking do that. I have other plans for her. Plans that involve using her just to fuck with him.

"First door on the right. Callie's room. Don't steal her shit," I call after her.

She shoots me the bird before disappearing into her room. I scrub my palm down my face and grit my teeth. I'd expected some shy, innocent little thing. Someone easy to fuck with. Not curves and legs and ass and sassy as fuck attitude.

I'm still standing in the middle of the living room when she comes out of the room a few minutes later. Her jacket is gone and I'm awarded too much visual access to her tits. She's no longer wearing her boots. Walking in just her socks, she admires my space.

"Wow," she says in a soft voice as she reaches the window. "This is quite the view."

I can see her reflection in the glass and she's no

longer wearing the snotty bitch look. She's smiling at the scenery down below. Fuck, she's pretty. That's a problem.

"We're not done talking about the rules," I rumble as I approach.

Her wide brown eyes dart up to meet mine in the glass. I don't stop until I'm inches from her. Another step and she'd know just how much she turns me on.

"I don't follow rules well," she bites out.

The urge to touch her is strong, so I settle my palms on her shoulders. Tension melts away in her body as she relaxes. Leaning forward, I inhale her hair.

"Here you do. I wouldn't want to have to punish you for disobeying," I murmur, my thumbs rubbing into her back of their own accord.

"Out with it, August," she says coolly. "What are your rules?"

The way she says my name in such a familiar way has some of my control slipping. My hands tremble with the urge to spin her and kiss her pouty fucking mouth. Goddamn, I need to get laid. And not by her. Definitely not by her.

"Clean up after yourself," I tell her in gruff tone.

"Got it," she snips. "Easy. What else?"

"You have to clean up after me too. Laundry. Dishes. Cook. The works. Earn your keep, little Winter."

She breaks from my hold and turns to face me. Her expression is fierce and she tilts her head up to stare at me. "I'm a neat freak. I can live with that. But cook? Hope you like cereal."

"You can learn," I tell her in a bored tone. "Like all the other adults of the world. Think of it as practice. So you can be a good little wife one day." My eyes roam over her cute nose and full, sexy lips.

She rolls her eyes. "You're condescending as hell, you know that?"

My lips turn up in a devilish grin. "It's what makes me a fucking monster in the courtroom. It's what makes me successful in life."

"Do you like being an attorney?" she asks, genuinely curious.

A frown chases away my smile. "It's my job."

"But do you *like* it?"

"I love it," I bite out. "Now for my final rule. No boys."

She snorts. "Don't worry. I don't do boys." Her pink tongue darts out to lick her lips in an inviting way. "I do men."

Heat burns through me at her words. My hand shoots up and I grip her jaw, shocking us both. Fire blazes in her chocolate eyes when I pull on her jaw, parting her mouth. Dropping my attention there, I roam my gaze over her wet, parted lips. I imagine for a moment what it'd feel like to kiss her supple mouth. She smells like cinnamon. I bet she tastes like Christmas and Hell all wrapped up in one deliciously sinful treat.

"You're far too mouthy for my liking," I growl. "I'm dying to punish you for it. In fact…" I slide my thumb over her bottom lip before searing her eyes with mine. Then, I push my thumb past her lips, loving her gasp of surprise that tickles along my flesh.

She grips my wrist, and for a moment, I think she'll pull me away. Instead, her tongue runs along the underside of my thumb. My cock jerks in my slacks and a groan of pleasure rumbles through me. With her eyes never leaving mine, she wraps those fat, juicy lips around my thumb and slides up and down as though I'm her own personal lollipop. I'm so stunned by her bold move that I jerk my hand away, the pop of my thumb leaving her mouth the only sound in the room.

Her smile is positively wicked and taunting as

she steps forward, twists her fist in my necktie, and pulls me close to her. "I like things in my mouth," she says with a sultry, husky purr. "So if you're trying to punish me, don't give me a reward instead." Then, the sexy look fades as she pierces me with a sharp stare. "And the next time you think you can intimidate me with your misogynistic bullshit, think again." Her lips turn up in a devious grin. "I'm not like most women. I bite back."

With those words, she turns on her heel, shaking her ass along the way. I draw my thumb to my lips and run my tongue along the wet flesh. Cinnamon and Hell. Just how I knew she'd taste.

Looks like Christmas is coming early this year.

And my gift is a naughty girl…one I'm going to take immense pleasure in punishing the fuck out of.

TWO

Winter

L ast night I managed to avoid him and spent the entire evening studying. It wasn't until I heard his shower running on the other side of the wall that I was able to relax. Callie warned me August was a dick these days, but she didn't warn me he'd turn my insides to a messy pile of goo. Sure, I'd crushed on him when I was younger. It was a silly infatuation. So I'd thought. The moment I laid eyes on him yesterday, I realized it was more than infatuation.

My attraction to him almost had me attempting breakfast this morning. But I can't even figure out his coffee machine. I don't have to be at school for two hours and if I don't get coffee, I'm going to murder someone. The only eligible candidate is probably still sleeping in the other room, and based on what an asshole he was yesterday, I'm not opposed to it.

Before I can carry out plans of said murder, his deep, rumbly voice startles me.

"That's not acceptable either," he says gruffly.

I whip around and the second I see him, I realize what a mistake that was. He's already dressed impeccably. His jacket is missing, but he dons a crisp white button-down and a pale gray vest that matches his slacks. The dress shoes he wears are shiny and match his black belt. His tie is a pale pink color. Only August Miller could get away with such a color.

"What?" I ask in confusion.

His gaze slowly rakes down my neck, lingers at my tits, and then travels the rest of the way down. "Your clothes," he grumbles. "Or should I say, lack thereof."

"I didn't expect you to be up so early," I say with a huff, crossing my arms over my chest. The thin T-shirt feels thinner than usual considering I don't have a bra on and my short silky shorts reveal just about everything. I'm feeling too exposed around a man who looks that good.

"I'm always up this early," he bites back as he starts messing with the coffee machine. I watch with rapt attention so I don't have to ask him again.

But I soon lose interest in his task as my gaze falls to his ass. His slacks hug his ass that looks too good for this early in the morning. I haven't had coffee yet, so I can't be responsible for my crazy thoughts.

The coffee starts brewing and he turns, leaning his hip against the counter as he regards me. I can't help but notice the bulge in his slacks. My flesh heats and I bite on my bottom lip to keep from letting out a girly sigh. I jerk my eyes up to meet his blazing green ones. His dark brown hair has been stylishly gelled in a way not many men can pull off. Just-fucked meets boardroom boss is the style he's sporting. Every male part of him screams to the female parts of me. But it's a lost cause. My dad fucked him over. And the evil glint in his eyes says he wants to return the favor.

I'll be damned if I'm anyone's revenge fuck.

"Cereal's in the cabinet," I say curtly.

His nostrils flare. "I don't eat breakfast."

I gape at him. The little monster wanted me to cook and he doesn't even eat it. "A little early for the bullshit," I say as I stand on my toes to reach an upper cabinet.

His touch is gentle on the small of my back as he steps close and pulls a mug out for me. I grumble out my thanks while he grabs one for himself.

Like two greedy little birds waiting for a worm, we hover near the coffee pot. Once the pot finishes brewing, he pours some into each of our mugs.

"Sugar?"

I jerk my head his way. "What?"

"Want sugar?"

Shaking my head, I take a step away from his burning proximity. "I like my coffee black." I smirk at him. "Like my soul."

This earns me a twitch of the corner of his mouth. Like he might have smiled but then thought better of it.

"Be ready in an hour," he says, his eyes darting behind me. "It's snowing pretty hard. You don't need to drive in this shit. I'll give you a ride."

I turn and frown at the windows. "I can manage," I lie. I hate driving in the snow. Yesterday, it'd barely started, and I slipped all over the place.

His body heat burns into me from behind. I bite back a gasp when I feel his hardness brush against me. "No, you can't," he murmurs, his hot breath tickling my hair. "I need you to arrive in one piece."

"Why?"

He twists an unruly strand of my hair around his finger and tugs. "Because if you weren't here, who else would I give a hard time?"

I want to blurt out that he needs to go bug someone else, but truth is, a tiny thrill shoots through me. Something forbidden and dirty. Callie would kill me if I fucked her dad, but man would that be fun.

Until he opened his mouth and slung out his insults.

"I'll be ready," I snip. "Thank you."

Two hours later and I'm staring at the board of my pre-calculus class wanting to jump out the window. Coach Long, while super easy on the eyes, is almost as mean as August Miller. Coach snaps and barks and grumbles to anyone who will listen. It just makes me long to see August again. We'd managed a morning without killing or fucking each other, which seemed like quite the feat if you ask me.

"Miss Burke," Coach barks out.

"Yep," I grumble. "I'm here."

He crosses his arms over his chest and glowers at me. "Lose the attitude."

This guy. Seriously. I arch my brow at him.

"Define attitude. I'm unclear if it was a good one or a bad one."

His jaw clenches. "I don't have time for spoiled brats not paying attention in my class."

"And I'm so over assholes," I mutter under my breath.

But apparently not quietly enough.

"Out," he barks. "Take your bad attitude down to Renner and let him deal with you."

Huffing loudly and ignoring the sniggers of the other students, I gather my shit and push past him. Tears burn my eyes, but I blink them away. I don't want him to call my dad. If Principal Renner calls him, he'll see what I've been trying to hide from everyone.

Dad doesn't care.

My chest aches at that thought, but it's true. Dad and I fought hard the other day, and he kicked me out. Sided with *that woman* and told me to pack my shit. I sat in my room for a good half hour, waiting for it to blow over. It didn't blow over, though. They meant it. My father chose his skanky wife over me and forced me out. It makes me miss Mom. She died when I was younger and I hardly remember her. But she always smiled in the pictures and it reached her eyes. Mom was lovely and good and wonderful. Unlike the one Dad married next.

By the time I reach the office, Renner is waiting for me. He's hot for a principal but nothing about his disappointed face is doing it for me right now. I follow him into his office and plop down in a chair across from his desk.

"Coach Long said you were disrupting his class," Principal Renner says, frowning. "You're on track for being valedictorian. You know better than to act out and curse in class, Winter. And yet this is the third time in a week that you've been here from smarting off to teachers."

Shrugging, I stare out the window. "Sorry."

"I'm going to call your father and—"

"Can you, uh, call Callie Miller's dad instead? Mine's out of town. She's my stepsister." My voice shakes with my lie. Renner sniffs it out but nods as he dials the number.

"August," he greets. "How you doing, man?"

I can hear the deep rumbling of August's voice coming through the line.

"Actually," Renner says, "it's not Callie. It's Winter."

A beat of silence.

Renner continues. "She said her dad was out of

town and that I ought to call you. She was disrupting Coach Long's class and got sent to the office. In-school suspension is punishment for the third offense." He darts his eyes my way. "Of course. Here she is."

I take the phone and bring it to my ear. "Hello?"

"You're being a bad girl and too afraid to call Daddy, hmmm?"

Swallowing, I avoid Renner's stare and look out the window. "Something like that."

"Are you going to be good for the rest of the day?" he asks.

"Yeah," I grumble.

"Then I'll get you out of trouble," he murmurs. "But don't think you'll go unpunished once you get home."

The last thing I need is to get suspended. I don't want that crap on my record. These scholarships are important, especially now that Dad is done with me.

"Just like that?" I ask.

August chuckles and it warms me to my core. "I can make it go away just like that. I'm good at that sort of thing. But it won't go without a price. Question is, are you willing to pay it?"

When Renner pulls out the in-school suspension form, my heart races.

"Yes, I agree. Just help."

"Put Adam back on the phone," he orders in that bossy lawyer tone he has down pat.

I hand the phone back and Principal Renner frowns. He nods a few times and then grunts out his agreement. My heart flops when he places the form back in his filing cabinet. Once he hangs up, he shrugs.

"I'm giving you one more chance, Winter. Don't screw it up."

The ride home from school, I try to get a read from August. He's quiet and calm. I don't get the usual razzing from him. It unnerves me. I agreed to punishment. He'll probably make me do something stupid like scrub his already immaculate baseboards. He's silent as we park and ride up the elevator. I want to go hide out in Callie's room, but just as I make a beeline for the door, he stops me.

"Drop your things off. Get into something comfortable. Then, come in the living room so we can talk," he instructs.

Just yesterday I would've balked at his orders, but I feel like I owe him right now. He saved my ass from getting in-school suspension and if I have to do some menial task to make him happy, I will. And if I have to do it while biting my tongue, so be it. I can handle anything he sends my way.

I change into an oversized black sweatshirt and a pair of gray shorts that say "PINK" across the butt. My socks are rainbow-striped knee-highs that don't match my outfit, but I don't care. If I'm going to have to clean, I don't have to look pretty doing it.

By the time I enter the living room, August has lost his jacket and tie. His sleeves have been rolled up, revealing his toned forearms.

"Okay, I'm ready," I say, looking around. Whatever it is he'll have me do won't be hard because his condo is flawless. Maybe he'll make me clean Callie's messy room. Honestly, I wouldn't mind organizing all her crap.

He starts unbuckling his belt, a wicked glint in his eyes, and I freeze. Of all the times I imagined rolling around in the sheets with him, never did I think it would actually happen. But instead of removing his pants, he yanks out his belt with a swish. I stare with my jaw practically unhinged when he wraps the leather around his fist.

"Bend over the back of the couch," he instructs, his voice cold. "I get to punish your ass for saving your ass."

My heart stammers in my chest. "You're going to spank me?"

His grin is wolfish. "Your worthless daddy never did. Someone has to step up and be the man where you're concerned."

I clench my jaw, my first inclination to defend my dad, but then I remember why I'm here. With a challenging stare, I waltz over to the back of the couch and bend over the back of it, making sure to watch him over my shoulder. His eyes rake over my ass, lust burning in them. I push my ass out further to tease him. If I'm getting punished, I may as well punish him too.

"Should I pull down my panties?" I taunt, hoping to rile him.

The leather of his belt rubs between my inner thighs. "Do you want to?"

Heat burns through me at his husky question, forcing me to look away. I'm nodding before I can stop myself. He doesn't wait for me to do it myself and instead slides his thumbs into the waistband of my shorts under my sweatshirt before dragging the shorts and my panties down. The cool air kisses my exposed flesh and I shiver. The material drops to the floor at my ankles and I step out of the shorts and panties. His sharp intake of air causes heat to pool between my thighs.

"I won't take it easy on you," he warns, his voice a deep rumble as he teases my naked flesh with the belt.

"I don't expect you to," I breathe.

Whap!

No warning, just a hard whip to my ass. I cry out in surprise, but then his palm soothes away the hurt. As I get used to his warm, firm touch, he pulls away and hits me again.

Whap!

It burns, but it's not horrible, especially when he rubs my butt again after. He stays away from my pussy and my crack, but I wish he'd venture over there. I'm practically dripping with the need to be touched there.

Whap!

This time, I choke on a sob. It's like I'm suddenly hit with the realization of my situation. I'm eighteen years old and I've been kicked out of my dad's house. He left me to fend for myself, knowing I don't have a job because I'm so focused on school. Knowing that it's freaking snowing and I don't have a place to live. He left me to the big bad wolf, although something tells me if he knew I was with his wife's ex, he'd have something to say about it.

August whips me a couple more times. The burn is nothing compared to the ache in my chest. The sob I've held onto escapes.

"Winter?" His voice is concerned and trembles.

Hot tears leak from my eyes and I try to bury my face in the couch so he won't see me break down over my situation. Nobody sees me cry. Not Dad or Callie. No one. I'm still trying to hide when two strong arms pull me to my feet. He twists me around to face him and then hugs me to him. I cling to his vest, trying to hide my tears of shame from him. When he grabs my ass and lifts me, I wrap my legs around his waist, eager for the comfort he is providing. He walks us over to a chair and then he sits, pulling me with him. I relax against his hard chest. I'm embarrassed by the fact I'm halfway naked and straddling his lap. His cock is hard between us and sandwiched between the lips of my pussy.

"Talk to me," he rumbles softly, his fingers stroking through my hair. "Did I hurt you?"

I shake my head. "It's stupid."

He grips my shoulders and pushes me so I'm forced to look at him. "It's not stupid. Talk to me." His normally cold expression is gone. Warmth bleeds into his features and I like it. Too much. It makes me want to snuggle against him and beg for more.

"I'm just upset…" I trail off, biting on my bottom lip so I don't cry again. I hate feeling weak. I'm Winter Burke, and usually a firestorm. Today, I feel like an ember getting lost in the wind.

"About getting in trouble at school? It's been taken care of," he assures me, his thumbs rubbing me through my sweatshirt.

Tears well in my eyes again and then a hot one races down my cheek. "Why did he send me away?" My bottom lip wobbles. "Why would he do that to his daughter?"

August's grip is gentle when he takes hold of my jaw. His green eyes blaze with intensity as he stares at me. "Because he's selfish," he says coldly. "But you don't have to worry. *I'll* take care of you."

I search his eyes. At the moment, all I see is genuine concern in them. It spurs me to do something bold. Gripping his wrist, I pull away his hand and then lean forward to press my lips to his. A small groan escapes him as he parts his lips, allowing me access to his mouth. The moment my tongue slides in and swipes against his, he loses control. His palms find my bare ass under the sweatshirt and he squeezes, pulling my cheeks apart. I shamelessly grind against his hard cock, slightly worried that I'm soaking his slacks with my arousal. We kiss hard and frantically as he grips my ass, directing my movements to rub against his dick. Each time it rubs against my clit, I let out a mewl of anticipation. It's been so long since I orgasmed. When you're stressed to the max, self-pleasure isn't high on the to-do list.

"That's it," he murmurs, nipping at my bottom lip. "Let it all out, sweet little Winter."

The moment my climax hits, I let out a quiet yelp, my entire body trembling with pleasure. My lips pull from his as I whimper out his name. His teeth sink into my throat as an answer to the call and he sucks me hard. Those strong fingers of his bite into my ass, pushing me hard against him so I'm once more on the cusp of an orgasm. His tongue slides down my throat and then he latches on again. I can feel his teeth and then he's sucking, bruising me. All it does is add to the experience.

"Oh, God," I hiss out as another orgasm steals over me, blacking out my vision. I crumble against him, depleted of energy. My nose nuzzles against his neck and I inhale his scent.

"You got my pants wet," he murmurs, his voice raw and husky.

I start to pull away, but he grips me tight.

"I didn't say I didn't like it."

His cock twitches at his words between us as if to agree.

THREE

August

I stare at myself in the foggy mirror and try to tap into my anger. What's wrong with me? I was supposed to be terrorizing this girl, not ripping off her clothes and dry fucking her in my living room. My cock jolts to life beneath my towel. Earlier, I held her after her two back-to-back orgasms, and then told her to get herself cleaned up. She was quiet as she ran off, her sweatshirt barely covering her red ass.

God, I am so stupid. I shouldn't have let it go so far.

But she was hurting. And dammit if I didn't want to ease that pain.

Exiting the bathroom, I find some sweatpants and pull them on. After throwing on a black T-shirt, I walk back into the living room. Pots clang around in the kitchen and it's a good reminder why

I allowed her to even stay here in the first place.

Fuck with her to fuck with him.

I tap into my new resolve as I enter the kitchen. She still wears the same sweatshirt but has changed into some black yoga pants. With her wild fake-red hair piled up on top of her head in a messy bun, she looks completely fucking adorable. All plans to irritate her fly out the window.

"What are you doing?" I demand.

She jumps at my words and shoots me a nasty glare. Fire in her eyes is even more beautiful than the tears in them earlier.

"Earning my keep," she says grumpily.

I chuckle as I approach. "By trying to kill me?"

"I hardly think a grilled cheese sandwich will kill you," she bites back.

"Grilled cheese?" I ask with an amused lift of my brow. "What are we, twelve?"

She rolls her eyes at me as she sets the pan on the stove. "Get the butter, gramps."

"Gramps?" I snort. "You have no idea how far from a gramps I am, little girl." Lifting the hem of my shirt, I show her my cut abs. I work hard as hell at the building's gym most mornings to keep this body.

Her brown eyes drag down to my stomach and

she licks her bottom lip. I'm grinning triumphantly until she speaks again.

"Is that a gray hair?" she asks as she shoves past me to the fridge.

Jerking my gaze down, I inspect my happy trail and run my thumb through the dark brown hair there. "There's no fucking gray."

She laughs, her tone haughty and condescending. "You sure? Maybe you should get your bifocals checked."

The little girl is poking the bear. Letting my shirt drop, I narrow my eyes at her. She's no longer teary and sad. Her smile is present and there's a pep in her step. "Make yourself useful and put on some tunes, grumpy Gramps."

I walk past her and slap her sore ass, loving the squeal that escapes her. I saunter into the living room to my stereo. Pulling my iPhone from my pocket, I plug it in. Flipping through some songs, I find a Lynyrd Skynyrd album. Old man my ass. As "Tuesday's Gone" starts playing, I walk back into the kitchen to see her swaying to the music as she butters the bread. I become transfixed on how cute she is. Everything in me says I need to fuck with her so bad she runs home to her daddy and complains. Truth is, though, I just want to fuck with her because it's fun. Because she gives it right back.

As she works on the grilled cheese, I find some tomato soup in the cabinet and get it started on the stove. For two people who don't like to cook, we work well side by side in the kitchen. I've had to learn from necessity after my wife divorced me. Callie couldn't survive on takeout alone whenever she'd come see me, so I had to learn to cook some.

Winter sings along and I find myself smiling, amused. Just like the storm that seems to grow worse by the hour outside, Winter blew into my world just yesterday and disrupted everything. And apparently, I'm a fan of the new chaos, because this is the lightest I've felt in a long time.

When I look at her, I see a bit of Tony in her, but then all she has to do is open her sassy mouth or smile, and then I'm forgetting who she is. Why she's here. Why I wanted to mess with her in the first place.

"Are we going to talk about earlier?" I ask as I stir the soup.

She cocks her head at me. "How you whipped my ass as a trade for getting me out of trouble?"

My dick jolts at her words. "And then after…"

"I shouldn't have kissed you." She flips the sandwiches and frowns at me. "It was a weak moment. I don't do weak."

Her body is stiff as she continues to cook, her eyes back on her task. Tough little Winter Burke had a vulnerable moment and now she's back to being the ice queen.

"You don't have to do that around me." I turn off the soup.

"Do what?"

"Act tough."

"It's not an act," she huffs. She turns off the stove and then shoots a withering glare my way. "I don't cry. So sorry you had to see that. You won't see it again."

"So you're not going to tell me what upset you?"

She was clearly upset over her father kicking her out, but I want her to elaborate and open up to me.

"You spanked me. It hurt." She averts her gaze.

I let out a huff of disbelief. "Little liar."

"Maybe I was humiliated at being naked in front of you." Her brown eyes snap to mine.

Snorting at her, I shake my head. "Try another lie, sweetheart, because these are shitty so far."

She presses her lips together and her nostrils flare with anger. Ignoring me, she puts the sandwiches on two plates and slams them loudly on the bar. Her challenging stare meets mine as she pulls a beer from the fridge, just begging me to say no so I'll argue with her.

"I'm not your daddy, Winter. I may like to spank you, but you won't find me telling you that you can't drink." I prowl over to her, forcing her to back her ass up against the wall. "In fact, I might encourage you. Then, your prissy bitch attitude might go away." Lifting my hand, I run a finger along the side of her throat. "And who knows? Maybe I'd take advantage of you."

I take the beer from her. With my eyes on hers, I step away to grab a bottle opener and then pop the cap. I drink a swig and then hand it back to her.

"Drink up," I urge, a wicked smile curling my lips up.

Her neck flares red like her hair. My cock lurches in my sweatpants in appreciation of the lovely color. She tips back the bottle and swallows. I watch the way her throat moves and imagine my dick shoved deep inside, stretching her pretty little mouth to the limits. There's no way I can hide my hard-on. When she finishes swallowing her beer, she roams her stare down my front and settles it on my eager cock.

She stares for a beat longer before meeting my eyes with fury blazing in hers. "I'll never be anyone's revenge fuck."

For a moment, I'm stunned. Then, I track the way her hips move as she makes her way over to the bar and sits on a stool. I adjust my aching cock and then grab a beer. This woman is going to make me crazy.

The music in the background is soft, familiar, and relaxing. But the little ball of fire beside me as I eat is bubbling over with barely contained wrath. It amuses me that she deflects with anger. I'd much rather see her mad than upset. At least then, she's a storm. Oh, what a beautiful storm she is.

We eat without conversation. When we finish, she does the dishes without complaint. I grab another beer and settle on the couch so I can watch the snow falling. It's coming down heavily and I worry it'll be a bitch to drive in tomorrow.

"I have to study," she says as she heads to Callie's room.

"Study in here."

She stops at the end of the couch and frowns, her palms on her hips. "What?"

"You're staying here for free? Well," I grumble. "I want something in return."

"Sex?" she asks, her voice shrill.

Yes.

"No." Lies. I grin at her. "Your company."

At this, she huffs. "Fine."

A few minutes later she heads to the chair across from the couch, but I shake my head. "Nope, here." I pat the cushion beside me.

"Whatever," she groans.

She sits cross-legged and cracks open a textbook. I skim over what she's reading and am surprised to find it's a book called Comparative Government and Politics.

"Is that typical high school curriculum?" I ask.

"Are you going to talk the whole time?" she grumbles.

"Yes," I tell her honestly.

She laughs. "You're annoying."

"It's the only reason I agreed to let you come here. To annoy you."

Her smile falls and she regards me with a tender expression. "To get back at him."

The old familiar sting of what Tony and Jackie did to me isn't as sharp. I shrug and sip my beer. "Maybe."

She leans her head against my shoulder. "I'm sorry for what happened."

"Yeah," I grunt, my body tensing. "It is what it is. It's been two years. I'm over it."

Her head tilts up and her brown eyes bore into mine. "But you're not. You're salty as fuck, August."

"What do you expect?" I snap. "My wife fucked your dad. Ruined our family."

"If it's any consolation, I hate her," she whispers, a flare of anger lighting her eyes.

It is, actually. Having someone to commiserate with feels pretty fucking good. I certainly can't complain to Callie about her mother.

"I don't really want to hurt you," I admit, my attention falling to her pouty lips. "I mean, spanking your ass was fun, but I don't want to hurt your feelings."

She takes my beer and takes a drink. "So we can be friends?" Her brow arches in question.

Goddamn, she's too pretty.

"I don't have many friends," I grunt. "Friends usually fuck you over."

Her brows furl together. "Maybe we can be something better than friends." She winks as she sips my beer again before handing it back. Then, she points to her book. "I'm taking mostly AP classes and some college courses. A scholarship is important to me now that Dad kicked me out. I don't have any other way to pay for tuition and I've worked so hard to get to this point. Getting suspended could have screwed with my scholarship opportunities."

"What are you going to college for?"

She beams at me, pure happiness in her expression. "I want to study law."

Both my brows lift. "You do, huh?"

"I want to become a badass attorney like my 'something better than friend' new roommate," she says with a laugh.

"You'd be great at it," I tell her honestly. "You're fierce and dedicated. And despite those tears earlier, you're not weak."

Her smile falls as she steals my beer again. This time, instead of drinking it, she sits it on the table. Then, she tosses the textbook to the floor with a thump. She sits up on her knees and straddles my lap.

"Take my shirt off, August." Her intense brown eyes burn into mine.

My cock jolts at her demand and I obey the bossy girl. With teasing movements, I peel away her sweatshirt. No bra. This fucking girl. Dragging my stare down to her tits, I grab a handful of each and admire the way they fit perfectly in my grip.

"You're beautiful," I murmur as I lean forward, kissing between her tits.

She gasps, her fingers sliding into my damp hair. "August," she whimpers.

Looking up at her, I grin. "What is it, red hot Winter? Are you scared?" I taunt.

"Yes," she admits, her voice a whisper.

I love that her tough girl act gets destroyed in my presence. It makes me feel protective over her. Like I want to shield her from everything the world might try to sling her way.

"You don't have to be," I rumble as I move my hand away from one of her breasts and replace it with my mouth. I suck her nipple between my lips and revel in the way she whines with pleasure. My tongue teases the peaked flesh of her nipple as I look up at her. "I'm going to make you feel good."

Her usually hard eyes shine with trust and admiration that does a shit ton for my ego. She tugs at my shirt, forcing me to pull away long enough for her to rid me of it. Hungrily, I attack her wet nipple with my teeth.

"August!" she cries out, her fingers gripping my hair. "Are we going to have sex?"

I laugh against her tit, with my teeth clamped on her nipple. Pulling away, I love the way she yanks at my hair, crying out in pain. I release her nipple and flip her onto the couch so she's on her back.

"No, little Winter." My lips curl up wickedly. "We're going to fuck. Have you been fucked before?"

She closes her eyes lets out a huff. "I had sex with a guy once…" she trails off.

Grabbing her pants, I start inching them down her thighs. "Once? I want more details, sweetheart. Thinking of you with your legs spread open letting some twerp take your virginity surprisingly gets my dick achingly hard."

"Why?" she demands, her bottom lip pouting out.

"Because I know the moment I stretch your sweet pussy and make you see stars, you'll be ruined forever. No other man will ever compare. You'll be mine and you won't be able to control it." I smile devilishly at her as I toss her pants away.

Her sweet, coy smile morphs into a wicked one that could easily rival mine. "Just once," she says, biting her bottom lip. "I was sixteen. Completely and utterly in love with my best friend's father. He was going through a bitter divorce and didn't even look twice at me. So, I found someone like him.

Let him take my virginity while I pretended he was someone else."

Bad girl.

Bad girl who plays bad games better than the big bad wolf.

She parts her thighs and reveals her glistening pussy to me. "He never fulfilled the fantasy. Sometimes, I wonder if that fantasy will ever be fulfilled."

I run my knuckle along her wet slit, loving the way she shivers. "Oh, sweet Winter," I croon, probing her tight channel with the tip of my finger. "All those fantasies are about to come true." My finger slides inside her slick cunt and her back arches. "And they're going to be better than you could have ever imagined, baby."

FOUR

Winter

O h God.

August Miller has his finger inside me. We're really doing this. I've only dreamed about it for as long as I can remember. With his eyes on mine, he kisses my knee and then makes his way along my inside thigh to my pussy. His hot breath tickles me and then his tongue is on me. I jump, overwhelmed by the sudden explosion of pleasure, and squeeze my thighs together, pinning his head between them.

He growls, pushing my knee back over. His teeth nip at my clit and I cry out. I've touched myself hundreds of time. And I've had sex with a guy named Hank—he was my first and only. But never have I felt pleasure like this. He sucks on my clit and quivers tremble through my body, making my legs shake. August chuckles against my pussy before he goes back to feasting on it. Another one of his fingers seeks entrance with the other. His fingers stretch me and then curl up inside me, finding a new button of pleasure within me.

"Ah!" I cry out. "Oh God!"

His sucking and licking and biting become more ravenous. He's losing control. I'm completely at his mercy. My eyes roll back when an orgasm detonates within me, sending electric pulses of pleasure zinging through my every nerve ending. His fingers slide in and out of me easier now that my arousal seems to be gushing from me.

"Look at you," he croons against my sensitive flesh. "Look at how your body loves to be touched and adored."

I melt under his sweet words. He removes his fingers and the loss makes me shiver with need. His green eyes flicker with desire and maybe a slight madness. The need to possess me gleams in his eyes. When his tongue darts out to lick his wet lips, I let out a groan.

"August," I plead. "I need you."

"Not here," he growls. "I'm not fucking you on the couch like some loser. I'm taking you to my bed where I can spread you out and take my time with you."

He slides an arm under my back and lifts me up as he stands. My arms wrap around his neck and my legs around his waist. I greedily kiss him, shocked that I like the way I taste on his mouth. Blindly, he carries us through the condo, his grip tight on my bare ass. Each time he spreads my cheeks apart like he wants to put his fingers there too, I shiver in anticipation.

One hand leaves my ass as he pulls down his sweats. Once they're around his ankles, he kicks out of them and then strides over to his bed. His thick cock bobs against the crack of my ass as he walks. We fall onto the bed and then his mouth is back on mine. Demanding and owning. He devours me in such a way that makes me feel claimed. I consider myself pretty independent but beneath him, I feel kept and cared for. And frankly, it feels nice.

"I don't deserve you," he rumbles, his mouth whispering over mine. "I am a selfish asshole. I don't deserve this or you."

"You do," I argue. "We both do."

He reaches between us and grips his dick. His tip teases along my wet slit. I stare at his wickedly handsome face as he pushes barely inside me.

"You're so tiny," he rasps out. "This is going

to feel so good for me, but, baby, I'm going to hurt you." As if to drive home his point, he pushes some more inside me. It stretches and burns as my body attempts to accommodate his massive girth.

"Ahh," I breathe. "I can take it." Tears burn my eyes because it does hurt. But I want it. Oh, how I want it. The one time I had sex was embarrassing in comparison. Hank sure as hell wasn't packing a monster.

His thumb rubs against my still raw clit. Wildness shines in his green orbs as he penetrates me with his gaze. "You'll take it," he agrees gruffly. "You're going to let me ruin this sweet, perfect pussy. You're going to let me hurt you so good."

"Yesss," I moan, spreading my legs wider, begging for more despite the pain.

His eyes fall back between us, his thumb lazily teasing my clit. "Look how your body wants to resist but then sucks me in." His cock stretches me more as he inches in. "You're so fucking slippery for this cock, baby."

When my eyes close, he pinches my clit, making my pussy clench.

"Eyes open, Winter. I need to get lost in them." His burning stare and the sharp angles of his jaw make him look like some vampire villain come to turn me to the dark side.

I want to go with him. So badly, I do.

His thumb rubs my clit harder, making me whimper in pleasure, and he thrusts slightly, pushing the rest of his cock into me. He's so big, I'm shocked at the way it feels so good to be completely filled by him. Like we are a puzzle that barely fits, but it's perfect. Our eyes lock as he easily brings me to orgasm with just his thumb on me. My body jolts as the orgasm quakes through me. Before I can settle from the madness only he can deliver, he eases his body on mine, his slick chest pressed against my breasts, and bucks hard into me. His mouth crashes back to mine. Hungry. Desperate. Unwilling to stop.

I claw at his shoulders and hold on as he wildly thrusts his hips in a way that has me nearly crying with happiness. I love being consumed by him. It's been a silly girl fantasy until now. Now, it's reality. The man of my dreams—the man I crushed over for years—is taking every bit of pleasure from my body. It feels good to give myself up to him. To yield to his demands and allow him the control my body so desperately craves.

His hand slides into my hair and he grips me to the point of pain. "You," he growls. "You're so fucking beautiful." He nips at my lip. "And mine now."

My eyes flutter closed as his thrusting grows out of control. His mouth finds the side of my neck, and he sucks me hard. I yelp, clenching around his cock. This seems to set him off because he snarls against my throat and jerks out of my body. Hot semen shoots across my lower stomach as he bites my neck. The loss of him is disappointing, but I love to feel the way he claims me by spurting his seed all over me. When he finishes, he pulls away quickly and scowls.

"What?" I demand, my heart stammering in my chest.

He sits on his haunches between my spread legs and runs his fingers through his messy hair, pulling at it. His cock drips with cum and if he wasn't acting so strangely, I'd offer to lick it clean. Fiery green eyes meet mine as he smears his cum all over my stomach with his palm and then over each of my breasts.

"This," he says coldly, "is not okay."

I stiffen at his words, hating the way my eyes burn with emotion. "Why not? It felt good."

His jaw clenches as he rakes his gaze over the mess he made. "Not the sex, Winter. The unprotected part of it."

Oh.

Ohhh.

Shit.

"I can't get pregnant," I choke out. "I'm going to college."

"You felt so fucking good," he growls. "It took everything in me to pull out. Another second and…" he trails off, his gaze hardening. "I should have wrapped my dick up."

"I'm sorry," I mutter.

His glare is murderous. "You're sorry? Baby, I'm the idiot here. I shouldn't have done that."

My body relaxes and I let out a breath of air. "Jesus, August!" I bark out. "You scared the hell out of me. I thought you regretted…us."

He slides off the bed and grabs my hips. Yanking me to the edge, he shakes his head slowly. "I regret almost fucking up your future. But I certainly don't regret fucking you."

His cock, still wet from his climax, slides between my pussy lips against my clit, but he doesn't enter my body. When I try to squirm to urge him in, he laughs and pulls away. He grips his dick and slaps my pussy in an annoyingly teasing way.

"I can tell your need for my cock is going to

be a big problem, naughty Winter," he says with a smirk. "So you're going to get your pretty little ass on the pill so I can come inside your tight pussy every single time."

I laugh at his possessive words. "You think we're going to do this again, huh?"

He pulls me to my feet. "Over and over again. You're stuck with me. Should have thought about that before you taunted your daddy so you'd get sent to me."

I recoil at his words. "I didn't taunt him."

"Oh, come on, baby," he says in a cold tone. "We both know your dad was a pussy. He would have never willingly let you go."

A swell of anger surges through me and I shove him from me. "Fuck you, August."

His eyes widen at my sudden outburst. "I just did, baby. Best fuck you ever had."

I shove him again, but the giant rock-hard statue of a man barely moves. Rage burns through me and I slap his chest. I slap and slap and slap. Tears burn in my eyes as I scream at him. A loud, embarrassing sob chokes out of me, which angers me further. My nails claw at him and that's what sets him off. His hand goes to my throat, squeezing until he pushes me away from reach.

"What. The. Fuck. Is. Your. Problem?" His words are punctuated and fiery.

"I didn't taunt him," I choke out, my tears shamelessly sliding down. "I didn't taunt him."

He releases my neck and yanks me to him in a crushing hug. I cling to him desperately, eager for the comfort. His fingers rake down my spine, sending shivers rippling through me.

"Shhh, baby," he coos. "I'm sorry. Tell me what happened."

When I don't answer, he pulls away and takes my hand. I'm tugged behind him as he heads into his bathroom. He turns on his shower and then he brings me in with him under the hot spray. I stand under the water, crying pitifully and feeling sorry for myself as he dutifully washes me. It only makes me cry harder. Once he washes himself, he grips my jaw and tilts my face up. He rains sweet kisses down all over my face, soothing away the hurt in my chest.

"Tell me what happened," he murmurs, concern etched in his features. "Let me make it better."

My throat is hoarse from crying, but I manage to rasp out my words. "H-He was siding with Jackie, like usual, and I'd had enough. She's a crazy bitch, August. You of all people know this."

His jaw clenches. "I do. I put up with a lot toward the end of our marriage for our daughter. Looking back, the affair was a shock, but the downward spiral of our marriage was not. She was a selfish bitch."

"Well, she hates me," I tell him bitterly. "Ever since…"

He frowns. "Ever since when?"

"Not long after we moved in with her, she went spying through my phone. She, uh, found a bunch of pictures I'd stolen of you. It was silly teenage stuff. I drew hearts on the pictures. It was obvious, my crush on you," I say with a heavy sigh.

His brows deepen together. "Go on."

"She screamed at me. Dad wasn't home from work and Callie was at cheerleading. She screamed and told me I was a whore. That now that you were divorced, I might as well go whore myself out to you. That you were just like any man, happy to fuck some young woman. I hated how she turned my teenage crush into something dirty and wrong. You weren't like that, August. I watched you for so long. You were good and cared deeply for the people you loved. I wanted to be in that circle."

He pulls me tighter to him and kisses my forehead. "You *are* in that circle."

My heart stammers in my chest as I search his eyes. His eyes never lie and those few words that mean everything to me are absolute truth. It gives me the courage to continue.

"S-She deleted everything. Then, she ransacked my room. There was a selfie of me and Callie that you photobombed. I loved that picture. Your smile was so big and handsome." I swallow and look away. "She tore it up and told me I was disgusting."

He growls and presses me against the cold tile wall. "Look at me," he demands. My eyes dart to his. "You are not disgusting. For her to shame you for crushing on an older man was disgusting. How she treated you was disgusting."

His lips press to mine sweetly and then he waits for me to continue.

"Well, from that point on, we were always battling. Every little thing I did, she had an issue with. Dad tried to defend me, but she always had a way of manipulating him to see her way. Back when it was just Dad and me, we were happy. The moment he ruined everything, he ruined me." I swallow back the tears. "The other day, I'd had enough. She was saying terrible things about you. About what a manwhore you were now, fucking anything that walks. That you were going through a stereotypical midlife crisis and she was embarrassed of you. She and my dad laughed. I was furious. How dare they destroy you and then continue to make a mockery of you?"

He glowers down at me but not with fury at me. At them. It warms my heart.

"I told them we were sleeping together."

His jaw unhinges. "What?"

"I told them they needed to leave you alone because the only woman you fuck is me." I let out a snort of laughter. "I went into some very graphic details of all the dirty things you do to me."

He cracks a smile and kisses the corner of my mouth. "Is that so?"

"Let's just say Jackie threw a fit. Broke all kinds of shit as she had a meltdown. Dad was furious, but I was happy for them to see how bad betrayal feels. It was all a lie, but, August," I say, grinning evilly, "I made them believe it. I made them believe every word."

I guess I did provoke my dad like August said. Still, it hurts that he kicked me out.

His growl makes me laugh and his lips press kisses along my jaw to my ear. The water contin- ues to rain down on us. He nips at my earlobe before whispering, "Looks like I'm going to need to know every single dirty detail." He bites my earlobe harder, making my nipples harden in response. "I need to know so we can reenact it all. I wouldn't want my darling little Winter to be a liar."

He grips my ass and lifts me. His hard cock rubs against my clit in a teasing way.

"You're going to fuck me in the shower?" I taunt. "After your little baby fit earlier?"

His teeth latch onto my neck and I cry out. "I did not have a baby fit."

"You kind of did," I tease.

"I'm looking out for your future," he grumbles, nipping at my skin.

"I thought older men had control."

At my newest taunt, it sets him off. He grips his dick, lining it up against my slick center, and then he slams into me. Not sweet at all.

"August!" I cry out, my head knocking against the wall.

"You play with fire, baby. It's like you want to get burned."

"Yesss," I groan.

He bucks against me in a way that's almost painful. But I love it. I love the way he consumes me completely.

"Touch your clit," he orders. "I want you coming and milking my cum right out of me. I'm going to come so deep inside of you you'll be pregnant before your feet even hit the floor."

I grip his hair and pull him back, warning him with my eyes. He simply smirks. Asshole.

"Touch it. Now."

I roll my eyes at his bossiness but then start massaging my clit. Our eyes are locked in a heated battle of wills. We both know he'll pull out, but I like making him feel like he might lose control and forget. He apparently likes watching me squirm, knowing I absolutely don't need to get pregnant any time soon.

But one day…

I stare at the most handsome man I've ever seen. He may have only recently grown attracted to me, but I've been utterly obsessed with him for years. I already love him. One day, I hope he can love me too. I hope we can evolve what's sparked between us and keep it burning for years.

And then…one day.

One day we can have a baby.

His green-eyed stare smolders into me, but it's as though he can see inside my head. It doesn't scare him away. A mutual understanding.

One day, but not now.

My orgasm hits me by surprise and I shudder in his arms. He grunts before sliding his cock out. His fist jerks at his length and then his heat splashes my belly.

"You pulled out," I say, faux pouting.

He laughs. "Bad girl."

"I do like you spanking me," I tease.

His features grow serious as he slides me down to my feet. He cradles my face with his palms and leans his forehead against mine. "You never let go of the idea of us together."

I shake my head. "Never."

"Good," he rumbles. "Because now, I'm never letting you go."

"Promise?"

"Promise." He kisses me softly. "Is the hard, mean little Winter growing soft on me?" he teases.

"Only for you." I smile up at him.

"Good girl. To hell with the rest of the world. I've got you now."

I'm barely able to stay awake in class. August has been keeping me up late into the night lately—not that I'm complaining—but damn does it make focusing on Coach's lectures difficult. I cannot wait until we finish finals and I get a break for Christmas.

I feel eyes on me and glance back at a girl I know as Jenna. Word on the street is she's a foster kid. My dad kicked me out not long ago and I have been struggling with my emotions. I can't even begin to imagine how she feels. She never had parents. It makes me miss Dad even more.

Her brows furl together when she catches me staring. Quickly, I look away and back down at my phone. I've nearly forgotten about her as I try to take good notes I can study later when Coach starts snapping. It's his favorite thing to do.

"Detention, Miss Pruitt," Coach growls out, his angry scowl for once not directed at me. "After school."

I turn to see Jenna gaping at him in shock. "W-What?"

"You seem to think laughing in my class and then sleeping through it is acceptable. Not in my class," he snarls before turning back to his lesson.

God, he's such a dick.

Poor Jenna looks like she's never had detention in her life. Her bottom lip wobbles as tears threaten.

"Are you okay?" I whisper.

She nods and bites on her lip to keep from crying. We're thankfully saved by the bell. I scribble my number on the corner of my paper and rip it off. Her green eyes widen in surprise when I hand it to her. On my way out, Coach glowers at me. I refrain, just barely, from flipping his surly ass off.

Coach needs a nap.

Maybe I'm not the only one who has someone keeping them up late at night.

FIVE

August

I stare at my email. It's from Tony. It irks me to hell that he's reaching out to me rather than Winter. Despite her tough exterior, she's hurting inside. Sure, she has me to help pick her up and keep her going, but the heartache from what Jackie and Tony did to her is still a fresh, bleeding wound. With a grumble of annoyance, I pop open the email.

August,

I know you probably don't want to hear what I have to say, but I'm going to say it anyway. Please don't hurt her. I know you hate my fucking guts for what Jackie and I did to you, and I understand that completely, but don't take it out on Winter. Callie spilled the beans she's staying with you. And despite what Winter said about you two having a relationship, I don't believe it.

She's always been one to say something outlandish to get a reaction. I know she's always crushed on you and probably wishes it were true. Your letting her come stay with you isn't out of the goodness of your heart or a favor to Callie. It's payback. And while Jackie and I deserve everything you want to dish out to us, please don't hurt Winter. I beg of you. This will all cool off and when Winter apologizes to Jackie, I'm sure everything will go back to normal. Just don't destroy my daughter in the process. She's young and impressionable. Not at all like one of your fuck buddies. I beg of you.

Tony

Fury rages up inside of me. There are thousands of things I want to say to him. Every one of them are hateful and cruel. Taunting even. And if it were anyone other than Winter, I'd let him have it. But something about her makes me want to protect her from everything…even a war between her lover and her father. She doesn't deserve to even be spoken about as though she's some fuck toy.

She's not.

She's mine.

I quickly type out my reply.

Tony,

Winter has a roof over her head, food in her

stomach, and emotional support. More than her
father is willing to give. Don't email me again,
asshole.

August

It would have been fun to tell him that she just
left my office after visiting me for lunch and sucked
my dick under my desk. Or how I took her hard
in the shower this morning. But what Winter and
I share is ours, not some insult to be slung at her
piece of shit father.

"Miller," a deep voice rumbles.

I look up from my computer and attempt to
scrub the frustration from my face with the palm
of my hand. "What?"

Dane Alexander, my friend and partner at the
firm, saunters in my office, closing the door behind
him with a brow lifted in amusement. He's used to
me being a dick. For some reason, he continues to
put up with my asshole ways.

"What are you so happy about?" I demand,
annoyed that he's smiling when I'm pissed as fuck
right now.

He holds out his palms and chuckles. "Retract
the fangs, psycho. Some of us are getting laid and
pretty damn proud of that."

I perk up at the news. "You're getting ass?"

His cheeks tinge slightly pink. "I am." It's all he says, but I sense more.

"Hmmm." I steeple my fingers and lean forward, resting my elbows on my desk. "Care to share?"

He smirks. "Nope."

"Then why are you in my office looking proud as shit?"

"I'm saving you."

"Saving me?"

"From Jackie."

I wince at her name. "What?"

"She showed up just a few minutes ago, but I told her you were in the middle of a big case. Then, I came in here." He shrugs. "You owe me."

Gritting my teeth, I lean back in my chair and tug at my tie. "Why the fuck is she here?"

"Beats me."

Winter.

It has to be something about Winter.

The only time I talk to Jackie is through Callie. She has texted me a few times asking for money for trips and shit for our daughter, but I never respond. Just give Callie what she needs. I hate Jackie. There's no reason she'd be here to talk to me other than to make me feel like shit over taking Winter in. I know my ex-wife well enough to know she's jealous. I may not be hers anymore, but she still feels like she has a claim over me.

"How's Callie?" he asks as he texts with someone, his eyes on his screen.

"Good. She's been in Colorado with her boyfriend and his family."

"Teddy Englewood's son Landon?"

"Yeah," I grunt. "He's a good kid. Both the Englewood kids are."

Landon is the football player to my cheerleader daughter. They're exactly the Jackie and I from back in the day. Difference is, my daughter isn't a cheating cunt. And if Landon hurts her…I'll kill that motherfucker.

"How are your cases going? Since I'm here, we could actually work," Dane says, setting his phone down on my desk.

We spend the next half hour going over a couple of tricky cases. Once he's decided that Jackie is no longer a threat, he leaves me to my work. Winter and I text throughout the day. Since it's now Christmas break, she's been binge watching old episodes of *Criminal Minds* and giving me a play-by-play on what's realistic and what's not. It's cute how much she analyzes that dumb show.

Five rolls around and I'm ready to get the hell out of work so I can take my girl to dinner. I pack up and throw on my coat before stalking out of the office. People don't even bother waving anymore. I'm a dick to everyone. I don't even care. I'm just exiting the elevator in the garage of the building when I immediately sense her.

My hackles rise to see Jackie leaned up against my Jaguar like she fucking owns it. No, she took her precious Mercedes after the divorce and my Audi. Since her argument was that Callie needed a car, I caved. I ended up buying my Jag later, so I can't say I'm all that mad about it. What I am mad about is the fact she's here and fucking stalking me.

"What?" I snarl as I storm toward my car, hitting the button on the key fob. "You have thirty seconds to say what you need to say."

She looks like the Jackie I remember. Sleek dark brown hair. Bright blue eyes. Full bought and paid for tits. High-maintenance as fuck. I hope Tony is enjoying every second of her awful ass.

"We need to talk. You can't rush off. This is important," she snips.

"About Callie?" I ask, turning my icy glare her way.

She bristles. "Callie is perfect. As usual. It's… *her*."

My brow arches and I grit my teeth. "Who?" I fucking know who. I want to hear her say her name.

She purses her lips before letting out a huff. "Winter."

Her name sends a rush of hot protectiveness scorching through my veins. "What about Winter?"

"She's trouble, August."

I let out a harsh laugh. "She's your husband's daughter."

"It doesn't change the fact that she's trouble," she bites back. "Listen to me. She has one of those creepy older man crushes on you. I've known it for years. That girl is the type to sink her claws in and go crazy if you don't give her what she wants. If you fuck Winter, you're going to get fucked. Mark my words."

"Is that all?" I growl, my words cold.

"No," she shouts. "It's not all. I'm trying to warn you here. She's going to obsess over you. More so than she already does. Next thing you know, she'll be pregnant. That worthless girl will drain you for everything you have."

At this, I sneer. "Seems like her stepmother

may be the best teacher for that. Although," I say as I yank open my car door, "she may be too late. I already had one frigid bitch take me for everything I own."

"August Miller!" she shrieks, her fat lips popped open in shock at my words.

"Fuck off, Jackie. Leave me alone. You already destroyed my life once. I won't let you do it again."

When I burst through the front door, Winter is nowhere to be found. I stalk through the condo in desperate need to fuck out my irritation. She's not in Callie's room or the living room. It isn't until I push through my bedroom door that I stop dead in my tracks.

A beautiful damn angel.

Fuck Jackie for insinuating otherwise.

Winter's red hair is beginning to wash out some since she's been staying here. And while it's cute on her, I like seeing her natural brown color return. She's wearing one of my T-shirts and my sweatpants along with a bright neon pair of socks. But what has my heart stammering in my chest is how right and sweet she looks on my bed. All the time this girl runs her mouth and likes to push my buttons, but at the end of the day, she's just a sweet girl who needs a good man to take care of her.

I tug off my tie and shed my jacket. As I pluck through the buttons on my dress shirt, she stirs but doesn't wake from her nap. I leave on my undershirt but strip out of my shoes and slacks. The lamp is on, but the rest of the room is dark. I crawl into bed next to her and like her body knows mine, even in her sleep, she curls an arm over my chest. I run my fingers through her soft hair and inhale her cinnamon scent that has permeated every inch of my home.

Tony needs to think long and hard about what he's done. I would never push Callie away in a million years. I don't care if she was being a little cunt like her mother. Never. She's. My. Daughter. How in the hell he chose pussy over Winter is beyond me.

My blood starts to boil again. In an effort to cool off, I grab my novel off the nightstand. It's a new one by Stephen King, and soon, I'm engrossed in the story. I make it through several chapters before I get sidetracked again.

Jackie needs to stay the hell away from me. I still can't believe I had to deal with her sorry ass today acting like she was doing me a favor. It's pretty fucking sad she feels threatened by Winter. Her insecurity was the start of her demise and the ultimate downfall of our marriage.

"The book must be scary. You're growling," Winter says sleepily, her thumb rubbing circles on my chest through my shirt.

I toss the book on the nightstand and toy with a strand of her hair. "So scary," I deadpan.

She snorts. "Liar. What's wrong?"

A sigh rushes past my lips. "Your dad emailed me."

"Oh?" Her entire body tenses. "What did he say?" A pause and then a huff. "Actually, no. Forget it. I don't want to know."

"Your evil stepmother came by the office, too."

She sits up and fire blazes in her brown eyes. "What did she want?"

Cupping her face, I admire her perfect features. "To warn me away from the wicked Winter storm that has invaded my life."

Her eyes roll so hard they may fall out. I laugh at her antics.

"Beware," she grumbles. "I'm awful. I already got rejected by one family."

I grip her hips and pull her across my lap.

"Don't talk like that."

A tiny tremble of her bottom lip is the only sign of her hurt feelings. Then, she grits her teeth and hardens her features. "It's true."

"It's not and I don't like when you let them make you feel that way. You're better than those assholes, babe."

She leans forward and I hug her to my chest. Her body relaxes against mine. Silent tears soak my shirt. I don't say the words again. She knows it's true.

After she's no longer sniffling, I tug at a strand of her hair. "You done crying yet?"

"I wasn't crying," she argues in her usual sassy tone.

"Good, because I don't like it when my girl cries. Makes me want to go kick some ass. I'm too old to be kicking ass." I kiss the top of her head. "Come on. Let's get up and go out. I'm hungry and you can't cook for shit."

SIX

Winter

"You're such a dick," I grumble and shove him when we get near his front door, making him drop his keys.

He laughs as he bends to pick them up. "Good thing you like dick then, huh?"

I swing my purse at him and he dodges. "I'm getting better at cooking."

"Is that so? Then why are we on day three in a row of having to go out for dinner? Hmm, baby?" He smirks at me. It makes me want to simultaneously smack it off him and kiss it to keep it on. Little asshole.

"We're slinging out insults now? Is that how it's gonna be?" I challenge, lifting a brow. "Why don't we talk about how old men need to rest between—"

His hand covers my mouth as he backs me

into his door. "I know you weren't about to say I couldn't get it up loud enough for the entire floor of this building to hear."

"Mmphk." I try and fail to call him a motherfucker.

"Because," he growls, his mouth dipping to my ear and his breath tickling me, "I don't want to have to remind you how I am always ready when it comes to you." He grinds his impressive, extremely hard erection against my stomach. "Always ready."

He nips at my earlobe and a shiver runs through me. His hand slips from my mouth and his lips replace it. I slide my palms up his chest over his coat, kissing him frantically. The man is right. Sometimes I'm the one who can't keep up with him. He wears me out and naps are my friend now. For a girl who usually can't turn off her mind, he sure knows how to flip the switch.

"When I get you inside," he murmurs, "I'm going to fuck you on that kitchen table we probably won't ever use again."

I can't help but giggle. He loves to give me shit about my cooking, but the little asshole isn't any better at it. His smile against my lips melts my heart.

The keys jangle and he drops them again.

Before he can release me to pick them up, the door opens from the inside. Both August and I fall into the condo. My ass hits the ground and the breath gets knocked out of me when he lands on me.

"What the—"

"Dad?"

August scrambles to his feet and I whip my head around to gape at my best friend.

"Callie," I squeak out and take August's offered hand. He pulls me up, but doesn't let go even though I try tugging my hand from his grip.

Callie's eyes drop to where our hands are conjoined and her mouth parts. "Ew, no." Her gaze darts to her dad's. "Dad, tell me no. Gross."

"It's not gross, honey."

She turns on her heel and storms off to her room. A second later, all the windows in the condo rattle when she slams the door.

August flinches before scooping up his keys from the ground, closing the condo door, and locking it. "I didn't know she'd be back from skiing already."

"Me neither." I frown as I dart my attention down the hall to Callie's door.

"I should talk to her," he grumbles as he tosses his keys on the entryway table and starts pulling off his coat.

Placing my palm on his chest, I shake my head. "She loves you no matter what. But me? I need to go let her know I'm not just fucking her dad to get at her mom."

He leans down and plants a kiss on my forehead. "Yeah? Why are you fucking her dad then?"

Because I love him.

I have since I was sixteen.

"Because I really, really like him. I want to keep him," I say instead.

My handsome lawyer sees right through my manipulation of the truth. His green eyes darken as his lips thin into a firm line. "Winter…"

I don't love you, girl.

Don't look at me like you do.

You're a winter fling to me.

Ever since Jackie went to his office the other day, I can't drive her mean ass out of my head. Anytime I'm feeling low or like I'm not woman enough for a man like August Miller, it's her inside my mind.

"Just let me talk to her," I say lightly, patting his firm chest. "I'll make it all better."

He pulls me to him and squeezes me in a tight hug. I'm not sure if he's giving the hug or taking one he needs. Either way, I cling desperately to him. His fingers stroke through my hair and he kisses the top of my head.

"It's a good thing you're a shitty-ass cook," he says playfully, "because here I was beginning to think you were perfect."

I laugh and give him a shove. "I'm going to be the best cook one day and you're going to have to eat your words."

Leaving him to taking off his coat, I hurry to Callie's room. I kick off my boots, tear out of my coat, and then push into her room. She sits in her desk chair swiveling back and forth as she types rapidly on her phone.

"Hey," I greet.

She lets out a sigh but won't look at me. "Hey."

I walk over to her and pluck her phone from her grip before tossing it on the bed. "Eyes up here, princess."

She sticks out her tongue, and just like that, I have my best friend back. "Why my dad?" she grumbles, but the defeat in her voice is there.

I sit down on the edge of the bed and shrug. "Because it was always him for me."

Her brows furrow as she stares at me. "You look happy. I was worried things would be bad, but you're happy."

A genuine smile tugs at my lips. "I am happy. He helps me not think about…" I trail off and emotion makes my voice grow hoarse. "My dad."

"I'm sorry they kicked you out," Callie says.

"I'm okay."

She rolls her eyes. "I can see that. It's still gross to me."

"It'd be weird if it wasn't," I say with a laugh. "Go easy on your dad. This isn't some fling, okay?"

Her eyes are hard and unforgiving, such a reminder of Jackie's cold stare, but she must see whatever she's looking for because she softens. "Fine."

"Now tell me about Colorado," I say as I strip out of my sweater and hunt through her dresser for a T-shirt. "You came back early."

"Lauren wasn't feeling well, so we came back. Landon wasn't happy because we were getting some quality alone time, but what could we do?"

I pull on the shirt and then flop on her bed. Callie and Landon's sister, Lauren, have gotten much closer since she started dating Landon. I've seen Lauren around, but never spoken to her. She seems nice, though. "Are you and Landon serious?"

She grins. "I would marry him today if he asked me. Of course he won't because he wants to make his dad proud and get college out of the way before settling down. But we both love each other."

"That's really awesome, Callie."

We chat about nonsense for a couple of hours until August knocks on the door. He twists the knob and pushes inside. His concerned eyes are on Callie, but he darts his attention my way for a moment. I give him a reassuring smile.

"Are you done punishing me?" he asks as he saunters into her room looking good enough to eat in a pair of athletic pants and a form-fitting T-shirt.

"Technically, I'm still punishing you from that Christmas you told me I wasn't getting a pony," she sasses.

He laughs and pulls her to him for a hug. "I bought you a Mustang when you wrecked my Audi this summer. *Technically*, I'm off the hook. Pony? Mustang? They're the same thing."

"Whatever, Dad."

And just like that, everything is all back to normal.

"You think Dad would like this one?" Callie asks as she holds up a dark gray tie.

I shake my head and point to the pink one in her other hand. "He's more in touch with his feminine side."

She snorts. "I'm not buying him a pink tie."

"Fine," I say with a laugh. "I will." I pluck the pink tie from her hand. We walk over to the clerk to pay for our purchases. "He's really hard to buy for."

"Tell me about it," she grumbles. "We're both getting him ties. How lame is that?"

I don't tell her that I already got him some other Christmas presents that are a little more meaningful. Like a cookbook for bachelors and several Stephen King novels since he seems to be such a fan. August really is hard to buy for. But, I like a challenge.

We pay for our purchases and end up spending the next couple of hours shopping. I'm burned out, completely out of it when I hear *her* voice.

Jackie.

I rode with Callie in her Mustang, so the sudden urge to flee is useless considering I have nowhere to go. All I can do is look down at the floor.

"Here, sweetie," Jackie says to Callie. "Just go swap it out for your size while I'm here. Then, I'll wrap it for under the tree. I'll wait right here and have a quick word with Winter."

I freeze at her words. Callie mumbles that she'll be right back. The moment she's gone, Jackie pounces.

"What are you doing?" she hisses, coming to stand close enough that her Louis Vuitton patent leather pumps come into view.

Heat creeps up my neck. I hate that this woman has always made me feel as though I were somehow a cockroach invading her life. "Shopping," I deadpan, snapping my head up to meet her glare.

She purses her lips together and I note the tiny wrinkles forming around her lips. Where August seems to get better with age, Jackie just looks old.

"Always such a little smartass," she snaps.

"What do you want?" I manage to keep the shaking out of my voice. It feels good to stand up against this woman.

"I want you to stop meddling in Callie's life. I understand that you despise me and your father." She pauses, capturing me in her icy stare. "And the feeling is mutual." This time, I flinch at her words. A satisfied smile creeps across her face. "But I will not have you destroying my daughter's relationship with her father."

I grit my teeth, desperately holding in my words. "I have to go."

"You can't run away from this, Winter," she barks at me. "I know you're fucking my ex-husband and it needs to stop!"

Several shoppers laugh at the mini war happening in the middle of the mall. I can't get away fast enough. Her voice, though, seems to follow me like a bad habit.

"He'll get tired of sleeping with you and then he'll be on to the next woman! You're not special, sweetheart. You're not special!"

Angry tears burn at my eyes as I disappear into the crowd. I pull out my phone and text August to come get me. Then, I text Callie to tell her I will catch my own ride. For the next twenty minutes, I hide out in Dillard's until I get a text that August is outside.

Rushing from the mall, I'm overjoyed to see his obnoxiously beautiful Jag parked right out front. He pops the trunk for me and I stuff my bags into it. The door gets pushed open from the inside. I slide into the front seat and jerk the door closed a little too furiously.

"Are you okay?" he asks, not making any moves to drive off.

I nod, hating that the tears are threatening.

"Is Callie okay?"

I nod again. "She's probably shopping with her mom now."

Those words have him cursing under his breath. He puts the car into drive and then reaches over to grab my hand. I bite on my bottom lip to keep from crying. Thankfully, he understands my need for silence. Instead of going home, he takes me to a bar.

"I can't go in there," I grumble.

"Says who?"

"Umm, the law."

"You want to be a lawyer one day, babe?" He flashes me a wicked grin. "You learn to know which laws are okay to break. Besides, it's a bar and grill. You'll be fine. No one is going to chase you out of there. If they try, I'll fuck them up."

I snort out a laugh. "Why does it get me hot when you go all alpha badass?"

"Everything I do gets you hot."

Rolling my eyes at him, I climb out of the car and head toward the doors. Before I can open the door, he reaches past me to grab it. He pulls it open for me and then slaps my ass like the caveman he is. I shoot him a death glare and he simply smirks.

"Sit anywhere," the guy from behind the bar says.

August grabs my hand and guides me to a high-backed booth. He ushers me onto one side before sliding in next to me. His arm wraps around me and he draws me close. I slink against him, closing my eyes and inhaling his comforting scent while he pretends to look at the menu. The bartender comes by to take our order, but I don't pay attention to what he orders. Once we're alone again, he kisses the top of my head.

"What did she say?" he demands.

"Stupid, untrue things."

"Tell me, Winter."

I let out a heavy sigh. I'm embarrassed to repeat her words.

He'll get tired of sleeping with you and then he'll be on to the next woman! You're not special, sweetheart. You're not special!

"She thinks I'm trying to destroy Callie through you. And then she warned me that I'm essentially your winter fling and you'll soon move on to someone else." I swallow down the bitterness burning my throat. "She said I'm not special."

His fingers slide into my hair and he grips me tight. Gently, he tilts my head up so that I'm looking at him. "Winter, I want you to listen to me."

I blink rapidly at him so I don't get emotional in front of him. Again. "Okay."

"You. Are. Fucking. Special."

Tears leak out against my will, burning hot lines down my cheeks. He kisses the wetness on my skin and then leans his forehead against mine.

"I would never hurt Callie," I mutter.

He pulls away and scowls. "You know this. I know this. Callie knows this. Stop letting that bitch get inside your head. Promise me you will just ignore her, babe. You're stronger than any woman I know and you're letting the weakest one I know get to you." He reaches up and tucks my hair behind my ear. "You're untouchable, Winter. And that's why she can't stand you. You're everything she's not."

SEVEN

August

"Try it," she huffs, holding up the suspiciously dark and hard cookie.

"Pass," I grunt.

She rolls her eyes. "It's good."

I watch in amusement as she bites into the cookie and crunches loudly. It's burnt to shit, but she's been trying her hand at baking on her winter break. So far, she sucks.

"Tastes good, hmm?" I tease.

"Fabulous," she lies. "You're really missing out."

"Did you chip a tooth?"

She flips me off. "No, asshole, it's not that hard."

My brows lift as I prowl over to her and pin her against the kitchen counter, my hips pressing against her. "I beg to differ. It seems pretty damn hard to me."

"Eat my cookie and then you can eat me," she challenges, a wicked smirk on her lips.

"You're evil."

She shrugs. "The cookie tastes good," she murmurs, licking away some crumbs. "But I taste better."

I shove the damn cookie in my mouth, my eyes burning into hers. It tastes better than her last batch and nobody dies unlike the last time when I thought *I* would. I call that improvement. As soon as I swallow down the last of it, I attack her throat with my teeth.

"Stop!" she yells, swatting at me. "We have that New Year's party tonight at your firm. Do not leave hickies on me, August Miller!"

"That's what makeup is for, baby. I'm marking what's mine."

"I want to make a good impression," she whines but then tilts her head to the side to offer her sweet, pale throat to me.

I suck on her lovely flesh. "You will in that hot-as-fuck dress you bought. No one will be looking at your neck."

She moans. "It *is* pretty hot."

"Red hot, Winter. You'll give every old man

in that place an erection. Who needs Viagra when you have a sexy woman with perfect tits in a tight, slinky dress?"

"You're disgusting," she groans but spreads her legs when I lift her.

"You're disgusting for liking someone so disgusting."

She pulls away so she can make sure I get the full effect of her eye roll. I laugh as I attack her neck again, grinding against her, wishing we weren't wearing so many clothes. Now that she's safely on the pill, I fill her up with lots of cum to make up for time lost.

She calls me a caveman.

I call her mine.

Our mouths meet for another kiss when someone bangs on the front door. I release Winter and frown.

"You expecting anyone?" I ask.

Callie's off with Landon and she doesn't knock.

"No. Were you?"

"Nope." I peck her lips and then release her. "Stay here. I'll be right back to finish this."

She grins at me and I burn that smile into my brain for later when I'm lying in the dark with that gorgeous girl wrapped around me, always dreaming of her. The person bangs on the door again and I scowl. I hate visitors. I flip the lock and swing the door open. I'm stunned silent as I gape into her brown eyes. But these brown eyes belong to him. The one who betrayed me.

Tony Burke.

My hands curl into fists and I glower at him. "Leave."

His jaw clenches and he looks past me, trying to peer into my condo. "Where is she? Where is my daughter?" he demands. He starts past me, but I block the doorway.

"She's been gone for weeks," I bite out icily. "Weeks and you've just now decided to come see if she's okay?" Emailing me or sending his cunt wife to my office to do his dirty work isn't good enough.

Shame flickers in his eyes. "I just want to talk to her."

The fire that used to burn inside me whenever I had to see this fuck's face is no longer raging inside of me. It would feel good, sure, to crush him with the fact I'm sleeping with his daughter. I'd love to see the infuriated way his eyes flare as he realizes I fucked him back.

But then I think of her.

It would cause unnecessary heartache and

stress for Winter. I watched for weeks leading up to winter break as she slaved over her books, studying her ass off. Once her break started, she began to relax and let loose. The poor girl has been stressed beyond belief. I'll be damned if I bring more strife her way.

"No," I say. "Leave."

"But she's my little girl," he rasps out pathetically. I see it in his eyes. He knows I'm not just fucking her, I'm loving her. I'm taking care of her in a way he'll never be able to. In a way he gave up when he sent her away.

"She's not little anymore. She's a brilliant, strong woman. If she wants to talk to you, she'll come to you. I'll tell her you stopped by." I start to close the door, but he stops it with his foot.

Her voice rings out as she sings loudly to "The Joker" by the Steve Miller Band. My girl loves her classic rock. That voice of hers won't be winning any American Idol shows, but it wins my heart every goddamn time.

"Tell her I'm sorry." He swallows. "And, for what it's worth, thanks for taking care of her."

"I always will." With those words, I shut the door in his face. I lock it and then prowl after my woman. She's standing at the oven, pulling out a new batch of cookies. These aren't burnt. I love how tenacious she is about everything in life. Eager to master it all. Even something as simple as cooking.

"Time to get ready," I rumble as I step behind her once she's closed the oven.

She rubs her ass against my cock through my sweats as she uses a spatula to put the cookies on a plate. "Ready for what?"

I hug her from behind and bury my nose in her hair. "For more."

"More of us?"

"I'm greedy," I tell her, my voice husky with need.

She pushes me back with her butt and then grabs my hand. "Lead the way."

With a grin, I pounce on her and throw her tiny ass over my shoulder.

"August!" she bellows, slapping my ass. "Put me down!"

"Never, baby."

I stalk through the condo and carry her to our room we now share. Like she's a sack of potatoes, I toss her on the bed, loving the mean scowl she gives me. It doesn't scare me away. It makes me fucking laugh. She shoots me the bird as I peel off my T-shirt. Her anger bleeds away when I push down my sweats and grip my dick.

She watches the way I stroke myself with heated interest.

"Like what you see, hmmm?"

"It's okay," she says, feigning boredom.

"Little liar." I edge closer to the bed. "Take your clothes off, woman. I'm not waiting to have you. Hope your needy pussy is nice and juicy because I'm about to fuck you whether you're ready or not."

Her gaze darkens. "Hmm," she purrs as she slides her hand into her shorts. "Maybe I'd just prefer to pleasure myself. I'm an expert now."

My cock seeps with pre-cum. This girl is such a fucking tease sometimes. I love that about her. Keeps me on my damn toes.

"Like you're an expert baker?" I taunt.

She shoves her shorts down and kicks them at me. Her small hand moves under her black panties. Goddamn, she drives me wild.

"Shirt. Off."

Her smile is wicked, but this time she obeys without argument. Those damn black panties are all that remains between us.

"Get over here," I demand.

She laughs. "Make me."

Her squeal is music to my ears when I grip her ankle and drag her to the end of the bed. I flip her on her stomach, then quickly snatch her wrist. Twisting her arm, I pin it against her back and the other one is still inside her panties.

"Touch that pussy, baby. Get it nice and creamy for my cock."

"You say the grossest things that somehow sound hot," she complains.

I chuckle as I grab her panties, pulling them aside. Her fingers peep between her legs as she massages her clit. So fucking hot. With my free hand, I grip my dick and push it into her tight, wet cunt.

"August," she whimpers.

"Yeah, Winter?"

"Come inside me. Give me a baby," she begs. Dirty fucking girl. We both know we're not going to do anything like get pregnant until she's done with college, but she loves to role play.

"Push your ass up," I demand. "Make me believe you deserve my cum."

She moans and attempts to get her ass higher. I fuck her hard and unrelenting. I slap her ass, loving the way her pussy swallows my cock whenever I spank her.

"I don't think you deserve it," I hiss out. "I'm going to jerk off all over your perfect, bouncy ass. Waste all that fucking cum on your pretty pale skin."

"Don't you dare," she bellows. "You're going to fill me up, dammit. I want to have your cum running down my thighs until the clock strikes midnight and you kiss me into next year."

I groan in pleasure. "You always have to win, don't you?"

"Yes," she croons. "Oh, God."

Her pussy clenches and I lose control. My dick spurts out its release deep inside her needy body. I love not having to pull out. The heat of my orgasm floods her cunt, satisfying the male beast inside of me. I love to fucking claim her this way. Releasing her hand, I fall against her, nuzzling my nose against her hair.

This girl is mine and she's not ever going anywhere.

EIGHT

Winter

I stare at the text on my phone and try not to burst into tears.

Dad: I'm so sorry, sweetie. Please talk to me.

I'm only a week into the spring semester, no longer stuck in the happy, stress-free bubble of August's condo. No, I'm back to school. Back to life. Back to reality. Coach's class is killing me and now I have Dad trying to make amends.

My fingers hover over the screen. The little girl in me wants to sob and fling herself into her father's arms so he'll make it all better. The woman in me, though, is angry.

Instead of replying to him, I text August.

Me: He says he's sorry.

He doesn't respond right away and I wonder if he's in court. I've just tuned back into Coach Long's lecture when my phone buzzes.

August: I bet he is.

Me: I'm angry but…

August: He's still your dad.

Me: Yeah.

August: Well, the offer to kick his ass always stands.

I choke on a laugh that has Coach whipping his angry glare my way.

"This is correct or incorrect, Miss Burke?" he barks out, his eyes narrowed as he points to the problem on the board.

Skimming my gaze over his calculations, I quickly reply. "The solution is correct because the four rational roots found are zeros of the result."

Someone snorts nearby.

When he goes back to droning on, I reply back to August.

Me: My knight in shining armor.

August: You mean your knight in a shiny, cherry red and chrome Jaguar F-Type.

I barely bite back a giggle.

Me: Midlife crisis much?

My phone buzzes again and I expect it to be August. It's a number I don't recognize, though.

Unknown Number: It's Jenna. I got a phone

for Christmas.

I turn in my seat to see the sad girl Jenna giving me a small smile. Once I've saved her name into my phone, I reply back.

Me: About damn time. I'm Winter…but you already know that because Coach yells it enough times.

Jenna: Ha…yep. This class is so hard!

Me: Coach's butt is harder. Seriously, you could bounce chalk off dat ass.

She sniggers but thankfully he's too busy droning on to notice.

Jenna: It is a pretty hard looking butt. I still think his class is harder.

Me: You think he's bad for a teacher…I heard he's even worse as a coach.

Jenna: Oh, God. I would die. I've seen kids running up and down the bleachers.

Coach whips around and starts yelling at a boy who's whispering to a girl beside him. I give Jenna wide eyes and she has to cover her mouth with her hand to keep from laughing. When he looks our way, we both play it cool. Eventually, the bell rings and we're saved from Satan's torment.

"Don't be a stranger," I tell Jenna as I shove my book into my bag and then shoulder it. "If you need a study partner or just someone to talk to, I'm here."

A smile tugs at her lips. "Thank you. See you around."

She hurries out of the class and I make my way into the hall. I'm walking toward my locker when someone calls my name.

Callie.

We've texted about silly things but haven't spoken much in a couple of weeks. She's wearing a frown and I cringe, knowing that eventually she's going to confront me about what happened with her mom that day at the mall. I got a free pass during the holidays because she spent nearly all her time with her boyfriend, Landon, but now that school is back in, she's going to say something.

"Will you talk to her?" she asks, her brows furrowing.

Jackie? Fuck no.

"Your mom—"

"Not Mom," she exclaims in exasperation. "It's Lauren."

I frown at her. Lauren is quiet and keeps to herself. I don't know that I've actually ever spoken to Landon's sister before. "Me?"

She nods. "She's mad at Landon, which means she's mad at me by default. But…" She purses her lips and looks over her shoulder. "She's not doing so well. Landon doesn't want just anyone in there with her. Please, Winter. You owe me."

I owe her for fucking her dad.

Uggghhh.

"Right, sure. Where is she?"

She waves me to follow her into the bathroom. Landon's worried stare meets mine when I round the corner. His shoulder is leaned against the door as he attempts to talk to Lauren.

"She's sick. Like sick sick," he whispers as I approach. "I want her to go home so Dad can take her to the doctor. She's been getting worse the past few weeks." Then he raises his voice so she can hear. "She keeps ignoring things, but this isn't something that will simply go away."

The way he talks to her annoys the hell out of me.

"Tell Callie to text me your number. I'll let you know how she is later. I think you two should get to class. Let me see if I can talk to her," I tell them.

He nods at me before taking Callie's hand. She mouths a "thank you" at me. I rap my knuckle on the metal door.

"Lauren?"

Silence.

"They're gone. Let me in."

The bell rings for the next class and it's then I hear the metal scrap as she unlocks the door. She's sitting on the closed lid of the toilet, her long blond hair hanging around her face as she stares at the floor.

"You okay?"

"Just nauseous."

"Pregnant?" I ask, frowning.

She lifts her chin and her brown eyes bore into me. "Kind of have to do the deed for that to happen." Her expression turns sour and tears well in her eyes. "That definitely hasn't happened. Ever."

I let out a sigh and walk over to the sink where I get a few paper towels wet. When I make my way back over to her, I brush her sweaty hair off to the side and lay the cold, wet paper against the back of her neck. "Okay, virgin girl. What's wrong?"

She snorts. "Virgin girl?"

"We haven't exactly been formally introduced before."

"Lauren is fine."

"Lauren is not fine," I say as I squat in front of her. "Lauren is sick, hiding from her brother and his girlfriend, and missing class. From what I can tell, Lauren is not fine at all."

"I'm nauseous because I have a blinding migraine," she grumbles.

"Why don't you go home?"

Her brows furrow. "Because Dad will make me go to the doctor."

"That's what people do when they're sick—"

"I'm not sick," she hisses, her tone defensive.

I study her for a moment. Dark circles under eyes. Pale skin. The heavy way she breathes. She's definitely not well.

"Not sick. Got it." I stand and pat her back. "Period pains are a bitch."

"Period pains?" She looks up at me in confusion.

"When I want people to leave me the hell alone, I tell them I'm having period pains and they need to go away." I hold up my hand before she can speak. "I know the truth, so you can't use it on me. But Principal Renner? He'll cringe the moment we start talking about periods. I'll get us out of here and take you home."

"Thank you," she murmurs.

"But promise me something."

"Okay."

"If it gets worse, go to the doctor. Whatever it is that's going on isn't going to go away on sheer will alone. You might need medicine."

She touches a silver heart on her necklace and a tear races down her cheek. "Medicine doesn't fix everything. Some things are unfixable."

I frown at her. "What is this unfixable thing? And how do you know it's not fixable unless you've tried?"

Her lip wobbles. "I know enough. I know what these things do. They take until they can't take any longer. Denial means it can't take anything from me."

Rather than telling her denial is a bad idea, I simply offer her my hand. "You can't hide from the inevitable."

"Right now I can."

Stubborn girl.

"Okay," I say with a huff. "Fine. Hide. For now, let's go freak out Renner. I can't wait to see his face when I tell him you're clotting and have made a horrible mess of your panties."

She giggles and I feel tons better.

Lauren is going to be okay.

At least I hope so.

As I try to focus on what Coach Long is saying, I can't help but think about Lauren. Yesterday, when I drove her home from school, I tried to pull information out of her about what was going on with her. That girl is stubborn as hell, though. I'll have to ask Callie to keep an eye on her.

Coach bends down to pick up his chalk he's dropped, showing everyone his fine ass today, and I peek back at Jenna to waggle my eyebrows at her. She's frowning hard but cracks a smile at my antics. My fingers fly over my phone as I text her.

Me: Why the LONG face?

She smirks and darts her gaze to Coach before looking down at her phone to reply back.

Jenna: Ha. You're so punny. Just stressed.

Me: Duh. You have bags under your eyes and you're twitchy. What's up?

She frowns and stifles a yawn.

Jenna: You don't want to know.

Me: I do…otherwise I wouldn't ask. Don't be so difficult. Spill.

Jenna: It's complicated.

I let out a snort, causing Coach to whip around and give the evil eye to every kid in this class. When he's intimidated us long enough, he goes back to the board.

Me: You're so grumpy and secretive. Lucky for you, I have the patience of a saint. Now tell me what the hell is wrong with you before I get us both sent to detention where I can spend an hour bugging it out of you.

The brat flips me off and I bite back a grin.

We ignore Coach's lecture as we text back and forth. She's finally opening up to me, but I feel like she really needs to unload. Texting in the middle of Coach's class isn't going to be enough so I ask her to meet me after school for coffee.

Me: I should get home to Cora.

Winter: I'm sure Cora will be fine for half an hour. Want to check first and let me know?

I stare down at my phone and curl my lip up.

Callie: You should come out with us tonight.

It's awkward being with her dad. We can't exactly double date because that's just weird. But she's also my best friend.

Me: Coach is trying to kill me so I have tons of homework. Raincheck.

She sends me some sad face emojis but lets it go. I shut off my car and look out the window to the coffee shop. My world feels so turned upside down right now. Callie has been my best friend my entire life, but lately, we're not as close. Since I can be kind of a cold bitch sometimes, I don't keep too many friends.

And yet here I am making time for a friend for coffee. Between helping Lauren the other day and now worrying over Jenna, I can't help but wonder if August has softened me up.

I read over his last text and smile.

August: I miss you.

He'd sent it at some point during the day. I know he's been swamped with court cases. The fact that he took time out to not only miss me but tell me about it means more than he'll ever know.

I climb out of my car and rush inside the coffee shop. In the corner, Jenna sits looking unsure of herself. She's pretty in a simple sort of way. Where Callie is the cute, rich cheerleader type, Jenna has natural beauty. Fire burns behind her eyes. For what, I don't know. I just see determination glinting behind her sadness and frowns. She's a foster kid with crappy clothes and no one who cares. I can just relate to her more than Callie right now.

Jenna is lost. I'm a little lost too.

She smiles at me and I can't help but grin at

her. A guy in a business suit blatantly checks my tits out as I walk toward the counter. I can't help but smirk knowing if August were here, the guy wouldn't have the balls to look at me. August has this aggressive aura that ripples from him. Protective and possessive. I love that about him. I mean, it makes him sort of an asshole sometimes, but he's my asshole.

I order a couple of coffees and then fix one of them up with cream and sugar for her since I seriously doubt she loves black, soulless coffee like me. Once I have hers a nice golden brown, I make my way over to her and sit down.

"Wow," I tell her as I sit and pass her the coffee. "You should smile a little more often. I didn't know you even could."

She sticks her tongue out at me. "Brat."

"There's the girl I fell in love with," I tease.

We spend the next half hour chatting. I learn that she's in a new foster home that she actually likes, but what has her panties in a bunch is one of the other foster girls. Cora. She loves little Cora and doesn't want to be separated from her when she turns eighteen soon. It's heartbreaking to listen to her talk about her, tears freely streaming down her cheeks.

As she goes on, I learn she has a major crush on her social worker, Enzo. And from the sounds of it, he's hot for her too. She doesn't need that complication in her life, but it seems like one she's actually happy to have.

"I'll do whatever it takes to provide for Cora," she tells me finally, her eyes no longer teary but fierce.

The fire.

It's for Cora.

I find it really shitty that the one person who loves Cora the most won't be considered fit by the system to have her. My mind jumbles at all the Ts she'll have to cross and all the Is she'll have to dot just to make that little girl hers. It's a good, solid reminder of why I want to study law. I want to help people who need someone strong and on their team to fight for them. Cases like Jenna and Cora are ones I would take in a heartbeat.

"My boyfriend's an attorney. If you want, I'll ask him if he can help you." I smile at her. August will do it. He'll see their sad story and want to help. He's a good man like that.

"Really?" she shrieks, putting Callie's cheer-leader lungs to shame. Suit guy nearby stops look-ing at my tits long enough to shoot her a disgusted look. "I'd be so thankful."

"No problem. Now tell me more about this daddy of yours," I urge. "You're like a walking Maury Povich show."

We chat for a little while longer as she spills more of the shit she's weighed down with it. Some of it makes me worry for her, but that fire in her eyes tells me she'll be okay in the end. She just needs a friend. Like me.

"You know," she says with another pretty smile, "you have a warm heart for an ice queen."

I shoot her a wicked grin. "Yeah, well, don't tell anyone my secret."

"Your secret is safe with me."

"Yours are safe with me too."

NINE

August

It's sad watching them grow apart. For so long, Callie and Winter were thick as thieves. Even after the divorce and things got weird. Callie and Winter were in their own little bubble of sisterly friendship. But now Callie's dating Landon and Winter is with me. I hate that there seems to be a divide between them, but I'm not sure I'll be the one to fix it.

Her phone pings with another text.

Jenna: Coach Long is a sadist. Thank God that assignment is over.

She ignores Callie's text while she replies to Jenna with a bunch of laughing emojis.

I like Jenna. She's been a good person to fill the void now that Winter and Callie have drifted some. It was a surprise when I found out the girl from school who Winter wanted me to help was the same girl I was already helping for a favor to Enzo. Small world, that's for damn sure.

"You have homework this weekend?" I ask, nuzzling my face into Winter's hair.

She sighs as she finally replies to Callie that she doesn't want to come over to a party at Landon's house tomorrow night. "Yeah. Huge report."

Liar, liar.

It's her excuse every time Callie invites her to do something. This has been going on for months now.

"You should go," I tell her. "Callie misses you."

Her body twists around to face mine. "I want to stay with you."

I kiss her lips that are red and bitable today. "Are you obsessed with me?"

It's a joke, but it's a reminder of what Jackie had said to me. I hate that woman and the poison she continually tries to infect everyone with. Keyword: tries. Callie seems fairly immune and I chalk that up to having more my personality than Jackie's. I'm immune because Jackie is a cunt and I have no time or patience for cunts. It's Winter and Tony who seem to have gotten tainted with her words. Winter is just edgy enough sometimes that I can tell Jackie's words fuck with her mind. And

Tony...he sold his soul to the devil because she's a nice piece of ass. I wonder if he regrets that part of that "sale" meant his only daughter was part of the bargain.

"I'm not obsessed with you. It's the other way around, stalker," she sasses back.

I lift a challenging brow as I reach between us. Her breath comes out soft and needy when I rub her clit through her yoga pants. "I'll let you come if you admit you're obsessed with me."

"Maybe I don't want to come, asshole."

I laugh. "You're a terrible liar."

She bites on her bottom lip and shoots daggers at me. Her hips roll with each of my movements, eager for the pleasure she knows I have to offer.

"Fine," she grumbles. "Now make me come."

"So bossy," I say with a chuckle. "Promise me you'll go to that party tomorrow night."

"You're cruel," she huffs. I'd think she was mad, but her eyes flutter as she gets nearer to orgasm.

"You like it when I'm mean," I argue playfully. "My sweet girl loves to be challenged."

She whimpers. "Mmmm."

"Say you'll go..."

"I'll go..."

I take her over the edge of bliss. My dick is

hard in my sweatpants, but I'll deal with it later in the shower. Once she's relaxed again, I stroke her hair from her eyes. I've never been with anyone like Winter. Not even fucking Jackie back when she was nicer. Winter is good for my soul. She soothes an ache deep inside of me that I never allowed myself to focus on before.

I know the emotion. I know it well. I just didn't expect to know it so soon with Winter.

Love.

Love sneaks up on you, shackles you, and takes you prisoner.

But it isn't bad. No, love is good.

"Come on," I tell her as I pull her into my arms and stand. "If you want me to make gentle love to you before dinner, I need at least two hours to make you scream in pleasure."

She laughs as I carry her through the condo. "Who said I wanted gentle?"

I toss her on the bed and she flips me off.

"Take off those clothes, Winter. I'm going to fuck you so sweet you're going to beg me to hurt you."

She strips out of her clothes and burns me with her best "come and get it" stare. Boy do I want to fucking get it and come. I yank off my clothes with vigor and then stroke my aching length as I admire her curvaceous body.

Her palms grab her tits and she roughly pinches her nipples.

"Slow and sweet and fucking gentle," I taunt.

She shakes her head. "And here I was going to ask you to put it in my ass tonight."

My dick jolts in my grip. I've slipped my thumb in her tight asshole plenty of times, but not my dick. "You always have to win, don't you?"

"Always," she breathes as she rolls over onto her stomach and then does some porn star move that makes me nearly come right then. She pushes her ass into the air toward me, sliding her palms along the bed. Then, she stretches back out, straightening her body. When she teases me with her ass again, I smack it hard.

"It's going to hurt," I warn her, my voice husky as I reach into the nightstand for lube.

She wiggles her butt at me. "Maybe I want it to hurt."

"I'll make you cry." I pour a generous amount of lube into my hand and then rub it on my dick. "Don't even lie to me telling me you want to cry. I know you hate that shit."

"Talk, talk, talk. That's all you do," she purrs,

pushing her ass back toward me. "No wonder you make a good attorney."

I push a lubricated finger against the pucker of her ass. "Keep talking trash, sweetheart."

She moans when I press into her. I fuck her slowly with my longest finger until she's good and primed. Then, I add another finger to the party. She squirms and I can feel her ass tighten around my fingers.

"Learn to relax those muscles," I instruct. "My dick is a lot bigger than this. And contrary to that mouth you run all the time, I know you don't want me to hurt you."

She's quiet as I fuck her ass with my two fingers. I try to add a third, but the way she grips the comforter and shudders has me stopping.

"Too much?"

"No," she lies.

I ease my fingers out of her and then playfully pop her ass cheek. "Come on. I'll fuck you in the shower."

"No," she grumbles. "I want to do this. You're not going to hurt me."

I shake my head as I grip her hips and pull her legs off the edge of the bed. "It will hurt, which is why we're not going to do it right now."

She rubs her ass against my dick and looks over her shoulder at me. Defiance shines in her pretty chocolate eyes. "I can handle it. I want it, August. I want you. Everywhere."

"We can try, but I really don't think you're ready, babe. No bullshit."

"Please," she mutters. "Just try."

I let out a heavy sigh as I grab my cock. I tease my tip along her crack as I pour more lube on her ass. Slowly, I press the head of my dick against her tight hole. Her breath catches, but she doesn't move away. It's fucking mesmerizing to watch her body stretch to accommodate my size. She makes choked sounds, but the stubborn thing refuses to tell me she can't handle it.

"It hurts," I tell her. "I can tell it hurts."

"Don't stop," she hisses.

I try not to black out with pleasure. She feels incredible gripping my cock. One day she'll be ready enough I can truly fuck her this way. Unbeknownst to her, we're not even close to being ready.

"Owww," she whimpers. Then, she grumbles, "Don't stop."

I bite on my bottom lip to keep from laughing at her bossiness. Slowly, I push into her until

I bottom out completely. Her body trembles and she's damn near pulling the blankets off the bed as she fists them. Instead of driving in and out of her like I want, I reach around to her front to touch her clit. She's stiff at first, but all it takes is a few expert pinches to her bundle of nerves to have her whimpering once more in pleasure. Each time she gets close to her orgasm, her ass clenches. I ease out a little and then push back into her.

She cries out. It's a strangled sound of pleasure mixed with pain. I strum her clit to the point of no return, enjoying the way she detonates beneath me. I ease my cock out almost all the way out. Just the head remains inside her.

I stroke the base of my dick until my nuts seize up in pleasure. I come inside her tight little ass with just the tip of my cock sticking inside. She whines at the burst of heat that's no doubt stinging her insides. Once I've drained my release, I pull out the rest of the way and smile at the way her asshole gapes for just a second before it clenches closed tight. It's raw and red and used.

"You're perfect, Winter. You're fucking perfect and you're mine."

She moans when I grip her ass cheeks hard and spread them. Her asshole opens slightly.

"You can't keep that cum in there forever," I growl. "You can't get pregnant that way."

A giggle erupts from her. "You're a dickhead."

"A dickhead who's going to stand here and watch you force his come back out of your ass. Come on, babe, show me how dirty you can be."

She clenches her ass cheeks and white, milky cum seeps from her ass. I collect it with my thumb and then push it back inside her.

"August!" she cries out.

I laugh at her outburst. "Turns out, I lied. I want you to keep my cum inside of you. I want it dripping out of you for the rest of the night. Every time you laugh or cough or sneeze, I want you to be reminded of me."

"I hate you," she grumbles as she starts to crawl away from me on the bed.

I pounce on her and pin her to the mattress. My cock hardens against her ass. "You don't hate me at all, sweetheart. Not even a little bit. And the feeling is fucking mutual."

My fingers run down her ribs and she squeals with laughter. It's immediately followed by a groan.

"Oh my God. It's really going to do that, isn't it?"

I chuckle as I slide my hand to her ass, rubbing

at the wetness there now. "Yep. And I'm going to keep doing this." I push the cum back against her hole.

"You're so damn dirty, August Miller."

"I'm not the one who keeps letting someone push cum back into their asshole."

She manages to escape my clutches and rushes into the shower. I stalk after her. We clean our filthy bodies, but our filthy minds forever remain tainted.

"Are you done trying to push me out of your body?" I ask with an arched brow.

"You're so gross. This is gross."

"You like it," I taunt. "If I knew you'd let me, I'd put my tongue there and taste myself on you."

She gapes at me in horror. "You would not."

"I would."

"Liar."

"I don't lie to you, babe."

"That's disgusting."

"Not to me."

"August…"

Her lack of words tells me she's curious. I kneel down before her under the spray of the shower and grip her hips. "Turn around and show me what's mine."

She twists and faces the wall.

"Bend over and put your hands on the bench," I command.

As soon as she complies, I spread her cheeks apart with my hands. I press a kiss to her asshole and then I tease her there with my tongue.

"Weird, oh my God, that's weird, August!"

"It'll feel weirder inside," I offer.

She groans but pushes against my hot tongue. The moment my tongue slides inside her on an eager hunt for salty remnants of my release, she whimpers.

"Wowwwww."

I slide out so I can bite her ass cheek and say, "It feels better than my dick, huh?"

"Oh yessssss," she drawls out when I push back into her.

She lets me fuck around in her asshole with my tongue until the water turns cold. Then, in a wild, feral frenzy, I fuck her against the tile wall until I fill her pussy up too.

I'll never get tired of having this girl.

Fucking never.

TEN

Winter

L andon's house is filled to the brim with people. His dad is out of town for work, so he's decided to go all out. It feels like the whole damn school is here. I'm annoyed that August isn't here with me. I'd wanted him to come, but that wouldn't have been awkward or anything. Callie would have died from embarrassment if I'd brought her dad to her boyfriend's St. Patrick's Day kegger. When he dropped me off, I didn't want to get out of the car. But he promised me he'd be back in a few hours to get me. He has some work to do at the office and prefers to do it when no one is there. I think it's just an excuse to force me to go to this dumb party.

Some guy hands me a red plastic cup that smells like it's been filled with vodka. He's plastered and it's barely eight at night.

K WEBSTER

"Drinksss on mmeee," he slurs.

"Pass, buddy. Not getting date raped tonight by a wannabe frat boy."

He snorts and yanks the cup out of my hand. "Frosty bitch."

I roll my eyes and slip through the crowd of people. I've been avoiding anyone I know for the past hour since I've been here. Including Callie and Landon. Last time I saw them, they were sucking face on the couch.

Desperate to get away from the idiots of this party, I escape down the hall on a hunt for a quiet place to call August. I end up pushing into a room that already has people in it. I'm about to slip back out when the scene before me has me pausing.

Lauren?

Two boys from school are kissing on her neck. Her shirt and bra are gone. I totally didn't expect Lauren to be into threesomes.

"Wake up," one of the boys says to her as he unbuckles his jeans. "Wake up so we can fuck."

Wake up?

Fury rises up inside of me and I charge over to them. She's passed the hell out. Her skin is pale and she doesn't look well at all. Did one of these assholes give her something?

"Yo, rapists in training," I snap, popping the boy on the left in the head, "get the hell off my friend."

The boy on the left scowls at me as he rubs at his head. "Go away, bitch."

"Yeah, bitch," boy on the right mimics.

I pop his stupid ass in the head too. "Get your asses out of here before I call Sheriff McMahon."

They stare at me in confusion.

"She's passed the hell out and you're feeling her up, assholes. Get it through your skulls. This is not okay." My voice is shrill and the urge to choke them both is strong.

Boy on the right stands up and stumbles away. Boy on the left is more stubborn. He stares at me with a challenge in his stare as he boldly strokes his dick.

"*You're* awake." He smirks at me.

Oh, hell no.

I grab a handful of his dark hair and drag his drunk ass off the futon. He bellows as I yank him away from her and then release him when we're near the door.

"Go," I snarl. "And put your dick away. It's embarrassing to look at."

He calls me every curse word in the book as

he stands on wobbly legs, shoving his unimpressive dick back into his jeans. Since he's slower than shit, I shove him out of the room and lock the door.

Lauren.

Dammit.

I rush over to her and kneel in front of the futon as I grab for her shirt. I quickly pull it over her head and push her arms through the holes. Once I have her covered, I try to rouse her.

"Hey, virgin girl. I just saved your ass. Literally."

She doesn't move or show any indication she's aware. My heart rate skitters in my chest. I quickly yank out my phone and call August.

"It's only been an hour," he greets, his voice gruff. He always sounds so grumpy when he's working on his cases.

"I need a ride to the hospital. I think those fuckers gave her something. I don't know. Something's wrong with her." Hot tears prickle my eyes.

"Callie?" I can hear the panic in his voice.

"No, her boyfriend's sister Lauren. Please, can you just come get us?"

"I'll be there in ten."

While I wait for him to arrive, I rush to

the attached bathroom and wet a rag. I dab it at Lauren's throat and temples. Her eyes flutter and when her brown eyes meet mine, confusion glimmers in them. I brush her damp, limp blond hair from her eyes and kiss her forehead.

"You're going to be okay. Tell me what the boys gave you," I urge.

She blinks several times. "N-Nothing."

Nothing?

She's definitely confused.

"They gave you something. You're completely out of it."

Her nose scrunches. "I wasn't feeling well… and…I don't think I should have drunk anything. I feel sick."

"How much did you drink?"

"Uh," she murmurs, closing her eyes. "Maybe one glass."

"They drugged you," I grumble.

"N-No, I poured the d-drink myself."

"Then what's wrong?" I ask, my voice a worried whisper.

A tear leaks from the corner of her eyes. "I don't know. I'm afraid to find out."

That day in the bathroom at school comes flooding back.

"You can't hide from the inevitable."

"Right now I can."

But not anymore.

My heart sinks because I worry there is so much more than what meets the eye here.

Hurry up, August. This girl needs a doctor and quick.

I pace the waiting room, my mind flooding with a million things that could be wrong with her. We've all been sitting here for nearly an hour. And it's uncomfortable as hell because not only are Callie and Landon here, both drunk as skunks, but so are August and Jackie. Callie must have called her mother to bring them to the hospital when August and I rushed out of the house in a mad frenzy with Lauren. Apparently, according to overhearing Jackie talk to Callie, my dad went to Landon's house to make sure everyone went home.

"Sit," August orders. "Walking around in circles is doing nothing but putting everyone on edge."

Everyone but Callie and Landon.

They're practically making out in the waiting

room while we find out what's wrong with Lauren. I love my best friend, but right now, I really wish she'd sober the fuck up.

Once I sit down, August settles his palm on my thigh to keep me from bouncing my leg up and down. His calm reassurance settles me some. That is, until I lock eyes with my nemesis.

Jackie's icy stare sears into me. Her nostrils flare when she glances down at where August grips my thigh.

"Whore," she mouths to me.

I freeze and August snaps his head up to look at her.

"Got a problem, Jackie?" he growls.

She sneers. "Just one problem. Seems you have the same problem, though."

Landon tickles Callie and she laughs loudly.

"Callie," August barks. "That's enough." Then, to Jackie he says, "Take our daughter home. I'll keep an eye on Landon."

Jackie hates being told what to do. With her and Dad, she likes to wear the pants. I know it infuriates her that her ex-husband still calls the shots.

Callie giggles again and it's enough to have Jackie huffing in resignation. She has to all but pry Callie from Landon's grip and then drag her away.

When they're gone, Landon pouts.

"I'll go grab him some coffee," August rumbles. "Keep an eye on him."

As soon as August leaves, a doctor with messy, dark brown hair comes striding into the waiting area. He's tall and ridiculously good-looking. I'd guess him to be around August's age—mid-forties or so. His green eyes burn into mine.

"Are you Lauren Englewood's family?" he asks, searching the room probably for an actual adult, and not two barely legal teenagers, half of whom are drunk as hell.

"I'm her sister and this is our drunk brother." I stand and walk over to shake his hand. "What's wrong with her?"

He eyes me skeptically, but one look at Landon and he surely realizes I'm the only one he can talk to. "We have her stable. She's doing okay. Talking with me and the nurses." He frowns. "Her blood pressure was really high. I want to run some other tests on her, but she seems adamant about getting out of here now that she's feeling a little better. Can you convince her to stay and let me run some tests?"

I nod and yank her goofy ass brother out of the chair. "We'll talk to her."

Landon rambles about how Callie and him are

going to get married this summer. I ignore him as I try to keep him upright. We follow Dr. Goddamn He's Hot down a corridor and into the emergency area. Behind curtain three, we find Lauren looking much better than an hour ago.

"Winter?" she asks.

"Is that any way to greet your sister?" I tease as I abandon Landon to go hug her. "How are you feeling?"

"Fine, but this guy is persistent," she grumbles. "I just want to go home and rest."

Dr. Goddamn He's Hot implores me with his glowing green eyes.

"Eh, sure, virgin girl. How about you take some tests real quick?"

Her nose scrunches and she shakes her head. "I don't need tests." She flashes me a knowing smirk. "It's period stuff. Oh, the cramps are horrible. And the clotting…"

Landon gags and stumbles out from behind the curtain. I hear him retching somewhere close.

"Mean sister," I chide.

She shrugs, unaffected.

"You're not on your cycle," Dr. Goddamn He's Hot mutters. "According to what you told the nurse."

I roll my eyes at her that the clotting excuse clearly doesn't work on ER doctors. "Stay for the tests."

"I'm fine," she practically growls. "Can you take this IV out of me before I take it out myself?"

He lets out a heavy sigh. "I'll let you go because I can't keep you." He pauses and shakes his head. "Promise me you'll follow up with your primary care physician."

She gives him the fakest damn smile ever. "Promise, Doc."

Everyone in the room, including Lauren, knows she's a big liar holding onto a dangerous secret. I just hope she confides in someone before it's too late.

ELEVEN

August

"We're going to die," Callie teases as she peeks around me to look into the saucepan I'm stirring.

"I know. Winter thinks food is supposed to be black before you serve it. Don't you, babe?" I call out to where she's tossing a salad.

"Yeah, fuck off," she sings back.

Landon laughs from the living room. My daughter hugs me from behind and stands on her toes to whisper to me.

"I'm glad you're happy, Dad."

I set down the spoon to pat her hand. "The happiest."

She pulls away and heads into the living room where Landon is watching a baseball game. Once Winter and I are alone, I tug her over to me.

"Graduation is next month. Maybe we should

have you applying to culinary schools," I offer with a smirk.

She rolls her eyes and mutters in a dry tone, "So funny."

"I'm kidding. You're the best cook in this house," I tell her, kissing her nose.

Her smile is wide. "That would be a compliment, but considering the other three people in this place can't cook for shit, I think that was still an insult."

As I press kisses to the face of the girl I'm super fucking crazy about, I realize I fall deeper and deeper with her each day. We've been playing house for a while now and it's the happiest I've felt in years. She brings light and joy to my dark world.

"I love you, Winter."

Her body freezes and she pulls back, her brown eyes darting back and forth as she searches my face. "Don't fuck with me, August."

I reach up and swipe a strand of hair from her cheek. "I'm not fucking with you, baby."

Years ago, she'd fallen helplessly in love with me from afar to the point she got her ass kicked out of her house. She never stopped. Her feelings for me were always there. As time passes, so damn quickly, I realize I'm right there with her. Falling.

My feelings may have come later, but it's no less intense. I've claimed her and I'm never letting her go. It's a promise I made with my lips now. One that is carved into my heart.

"I guess you're going to keep me now?" she says, grinning happily.

"I wasn't ever going to let you go."

I hadn't realized until I had this girl in my arms that she'd been the thing I was searching for these past two years. Bitterness and anger ruled my every thought and action. I'd been looking for something that didn't hurt. Something that felt good for a change. Winter felt better than good. She peeled off those awful layers and found me again.

"Oh, God, I love you too," she murmurs. "I always have."

Graduation Night…

"I'm so proud of you," I tell Winter, squeezing her hand. "Top of your class. That's my girl."

"And I'm chopped liver back here," Callie says with a laugh. "Three point four GPA isn't that bad."

"It's not that good either," I say with a smirk.

"Punk," Callie mutters back playfully before growing serious. "You guys going to be okay tonight?"

I will be. I'm used to my cunt ex-wife. But Winter is who I worry about. If that bitch so much as thinks about ruining Winter and Callie's graduation night by running her fucking mouth, I'm going to lose my shit.

"We'll be fine," Winter assures her. "It's just one dinner."

"Yeah, and you're not cooking, so nobody will die," Callie chimes in.

"Pity," I grumble, earning giggles from both girls.

We talk about a summer trip to Italy I'm going to take them on before they have to go to college. After this summer, they'll officially part ways. Where Callie is going off with Landon across the damn US, Winter is going to the same local university I went to. It was where she wanted to go long before we ever started dating, and frankly, I'm happy she'll be close.

I pull into the steakhouse where we have reservations for the five of us. Although, if all goes well and no one kills each other, we'll pull up an extra chair for Landon who may show up later.

Callie thought it best we dined on neutral grounds. I can handle seeing them, because I don't give a shit about Tony or Jackie. I just hope Winter is as strong as she thinks she is.

"Oh boy," Callie grumbles, her face lighting up in the backseat as she texts. "Mom's in a mood."

What the fuck else is new?

"Hmm," is all I say.

"All they do is fight lately," she grumbles as she responds.

Winter and I exchange curious looks as I pull into a parking spot. I climb out of Callie's Mustang. My Jag is just a little two-seater, so we had to bring her car tonight. Winter hurries over to me and threads her fingers with mine while we wait for Callie to finish rapid-firing texting to her mom.

"Jenna got a new car. Can you believe it?" Winter says absently, trying and failing to steer the conversation away from whatever Callie is grumbling about.

"That's nice," I say, also not doing a good job on giving Callie her privacy.

"Oh God," Callie groans. "Mom is nuclear right now."

I hug Callie from the side. "Don't let any of this rain on your happy day, okay?"

"I'm not worried about me," she murmurs.

I'm tense as we enter the restaurant. The server guides us to where Jackie and Tony are sitting. Tony's features harden when he realizes Winter's arm is looped through mine. Jackie is practically spitting venom.

"Sweetheart," Jackie says, patting the vacant seat beside her. Callie walks over and sits beside her mother. They launch into a conversation about Callie's dress.

Winter shifts on her feet. I could take the seat beside Tony so she sits next to Callie. I'd do that for her. But before I can sit, she plops down beside her father. The relief in his eyes is enough to have some of the ice melting off me. I hate him and what he did to me—what he did to my sweet Winter—but at the end of the day, he's still her father. And the expression on his face is one I know all too well. He loves her more than words could ever express.

I sit down beside her and grip her thigh under the table before leaning in. "You're doing great, beautiful."

She turns and flashes me a thankful smile. Jackie's glare is on the two of us no matter how hard Callie tries to distract her. Tony's eyes are just for his daughter as he attempts to engage.

"You looked amazing up there," he tells her. "I'm so proud of you."

She tenses and a strained smile spreads across her face. "Thanks." Her voice takes on that hoarse quality right before she cries. It makes me want to drag her back to the safety of my home.

Tony frowns at her expression. I forget he knows her just as well. He reaches over and takes her hand. "Winter, I'm so sorry."

"Tony," Jackie snaps. "We talked about this."

Callie clutches her mom's bicep. "Mom," she warns.

Tony ignores his wife to focus on Winter. "Please forgive me," he rasps out. "I was wrong."

Winter bows her head and swipes a tear away with the heel of her hand. "D-Dad." Her voice cracks and I squeeze her thigh to let her know I am still here for her.

He somehow manages to pull her to him for a hug. To my surprise, she goes willingly. I know this fight with her father has been eating away at her for months. If this is what she needs to be happy, I'll support her every step of the way.

"No," Jackie screeches. "I told you I will not stand for the way she spoke to me!"

"That's enough," I growl in warning.

She sneers at me. "I don't have to listen to you, thank God. But him," she snaps. "He has to listen to me because he's my husband!"

"Listen to yourself, Jackie," I bite out. "You're making a scene and embarrassing our daughter."

Ignoring me, she turns her wrath on Tony. "You can't have us both. Not when your daughter is a whore and—"

"Jackie!" Both Tony and I bellow at once.

"She is," Jackie screeches. "She wanted to fuck my husband when she was just a little girl!"

Tony releases Winter to turn on Jackie. A vein sticks out of his neck as he thrums with fury. "That's enough."

"I won't stand for this," she bellows. "Like I told you before, it's either me or—"

"Her," he growls. "I choose her. I let you fuck with my head before, but I'm tired of it, Jackie. I'm tired of you. You're an emotional vampire and I'm sick as hell of you feeding from me."

Callie and I share a weighted look. Jackie, completely oblivious that the whole goddamn town is watching this war at our table, gapes at him.

"I guess it's a bad time to tell you I fucked your boss," she spits out at him before standing and storming away.

Callie gapes at me, indecision warring in her eyes. I nod at her. Jackie's her mom and I know she wants to check on her. She rises from the table and rushes off.

"Ouch," Winter mutters. "She fucked your boss? Gordon?"

Tony snorts and takes a long pull from his beer bottle. "His problem now."

I laugh because I thought the same when Tony started seeing Jackie. Well, at least after I got past the initial shock of being cheated on. Jackie is a huge problem and hell if this guy doesn't seem relieved to be done with her.

"You really meant all that?" Winter asks.

Tony nods. "We were in a bad place. I was trying to save our marriage. When she told me her lies, I believed them. When she made me choose a side, I got caught up in trying to fix us..." At the sacrifice of his daughter. "I made a mistake. A bad one. I'll do whatever it takes to get you back into my life."

She hugs him again and he looks a little teary-eyed with relief. Winter eventually pulls back and straightens her spine. "Dad, I'm seeing August now."

"She's not a whore and I fucking love her," I

growl. "Got a problem with that?"

He grits his teeth but shakes his head. "No problem as long as she is happy and loved. That's all I could ever hope for."

"I learned how to cook," she chirps, her lie so sweet I almost believe it.

"Impressive," he says. "Maybe you could cook for me sometime."

She preens and I snort, which earns me an elbow to the gut. Tony darts his brown eyes that match hers exactly back and forth between us.

"She still burns mac and cheese?" he asks with a smirk.

"She burns cereal," I retort.

"Assholes. You are both assholes," she says with a laugh. "I hate you both."

Callie returns without her mother. "What'd I miss?"

"Winter is lying to her dad. Told him she's a star chef now," I tease.

Callie cackles and Winter flips her off.

"I got sick when she made spaghetti last week," Callie tells Tony. "Is it possible to get garlic poisoning?"

"Arsenic is my secret ingredient," Winter deadpans to Callie.

As the girls snap playfully back and forth, I can't help but feel somewhat relieved. Jackie will go have her bitch-fit elsewhere. Winter can repair her relationship with Tony. And we can have a nice meal that my girlfriend didn't cook. Thank God.

Landon shows up and tells hilarious football stories that Tony seems quite tickled by. While they're distracted, I hug Winter to me and kiss her cheek.

"You're mine forever."

"Sheesh, man," she teases. "You move fast. I think the romance books call this instalove. The real world would call you a creepy stalker."

"Don't make me spank you."

Her eyes meet mine, a devious glint in them. "Don't threaten me with a good time."

I tuck a strand of hair behind her ear, admiring how beautiful she is. She regards me with soft, loving eyes. So sweet and innocent and mine.

"For the record, I love instalove and creepy stalkers and a good spanking," she says, tilting her head, offering her lips to me.

I kiss her supple lips. "For the record, I love you."

EPILOGUE

Winter

Seven years later…

Oh God.

The envelope feels heavy in my hands. I mean, it's my future after all. I should just rip it open and find out one way or another. I've been working hard all through college and then law school. I was prepared. I know I passed, deep down.

Right?

But what if I didn't?

August will try so hard to cheer me up and then pump me up to try again.

Sickness roils in my stomach. I've been so stressed, I can't eat. I can't sleep. I can't do anything but obsess. And before that, all I did was study. It was taking a toll on my health. While I studied and studied, it was all August could do to keep me fed and hydrated. This past summer, I got sick three times in a row.

Something has to give.

Bile creeps up my throat and I try to ignore it. I feel horrible and I swear to God if I have another sinus infection, I'm going to go nuts. My stomach aches sending a cold sweat across my flesh.

I think of one of my close friends who dealt with some horrible health issues. Suddenly, I'm worried on top of being worried. What if passing the bar exam becomes the most unimportant issue in my life? What if I'm dying?

The door bursts open and Dad strides in, an expectant look on his face. "You passed?"

Instead of being excited about the envelope in my hands, I burst into tears. "I'm dying."

"What?" he says, chuckling. When he realizes I'm serious, he frowns. "What's wrong?"

"I-I need August to get home already," I sob. "I need to go to the hospital."

"Honey," Dad coos. "I think you're having an anxiety attack."

"Dad, I'm sick!" I screech, hot tears streaming down my cheeks. As if to attest to this, my stomach clenches and I nearly pass out from a wave of dizziness.

"Jesus," he curses. "Come here. I've got you."

He helps me out to his car and then he fires up his engine. I sit in the passenger seat with my unopened envelope now sitting in my purse. My phone buzzes and it's Jenna texting me.

Jenna: Did you pass? Are we celebrating with margaritas tonight? Dad'll watch the kids when he gets off his shift in another hour.

I swipe away my tears and reply back.

Me: Raincheck. I'm headed to the hospital. Something's not right.

She replies begging me to call her as soon as I know something and I promise that I will. Dad pulls into the ER lot and helps me out. As I hobble in to check in, I can hear him calling August. It just makes me cry harder.

Dr. Goddamn He's Hot comes trotting down the corridor looking like one of those hot daddy doctors from that old show *ER*. He's taken, I'm taken, and I'm friends with his daughter. I can still appreciate a fine looking man.

"I've got it," he tells the receptionist as he guides me past the empty waiting room into the first room in the emergency area. "What's going on, Winter?"

I tell him everything. The stress. The chronic

sinus infections. The anxiety. My failed meals that make everyone sick. I probably gave myself ulcers. Bleeding ulcers probably. Oh God, what if my stomach is filling with blood as we speak?

A loud, horrible sob rattles from me. He calls for a nurse who draws some blood and then guides me to the bathroom. They ask me to pee in a cup and then once I'm done with that, I settle into the bed. Both Dr. Goddamn He's Hot—or Dr. Venable if you want to get technical—and the nurse leave me momentarily. Dad stays perched beside the bed, a worried look on his face.

"If you'll just open the letter, you'll feel better," he says.

"I can't," I whisper.

He starts to part his mouth to say something, but the curtain gets yanked aside so hard, I worry it might come out of the ceiling. August, brows furrowed with worry, stalks into the room.

"What's wrong?" he demands in that filthy courtroom voice that never fails to turn me on.

Suddenly, I feel marginally better.

I think about how he woke me up this morning. With his tongue. In places no tongue should go. God, he is so dirty sometimes.

"She got the results," Dad tattles.

August frowns. "You failed?"

"Of course not," I snap. "Well, I mean, technically I don't know. But I know the law better than you. I know I passed."

Dad and August share a smirk. Then, August saunters over to my purse and yanks out the envelope. He rips it open. Just pulls off the proverbial Band-Aid. I watch his expression for any tells. He remains impassive as he hands it over to me.

I stare at the words, unbelieving.

Passed.

"You passed, sweetheart," Dad says gently. "Congrats. Now you can calm down."

But something's still not right. I twist my giant diamond around my wedding finger. It's a nervous habit that drives August nuts. He grabs my hand and pulls it to him so I'll stop my fidgeting. His eyes are unusually soft as he regards me.

"Tony, she just needs some water. Can you go grab her a bottle?" August asks, his eyes never leaving mine.

Dad nods and kisses me on the top of my head before leaving. August sits beside me and threads our fingers together.

"You know I love you no matter what," he says, his brows furling together.

A spike of panic rises up inside of me. Why is he being so weird? "Y-Yeah."

"I made vows to you six years ago that I'd be there with you through it all." He leans forward and kisses my forehead. "Even when you lose your shit."

"Excuse me?" I hiss, no longer feeling sweet and loving toward him. "I am not losing my shit!"

"Not yet," he mutters.

Dr. Venable walks in wearing a cheesy grin on his face. "Winter…"

Oh God.

"Here we go," August says to no one. "Five, four, three, two…"

"You're perfectly healthy," Dr. Venable says. "And pregnant."

"And the shit is officially lost," August says to me.

"I'M WHAT?!" I screech. "IMPOSSIBLE!"

August laughs, that dirty bastard. Dr. Venable simply shrugs.

"No! I take that damn birth control religiously!" I argue. Hot tears well in my eyes. Thoughts of carrying August's little girl or boy has joy chasing away all the anxiety I'd been feeling for months over this dumb bar exam.

"You did," August agrees. "But—"

"No buts!" I snap at him. Oh God, will my little angel have brown eyes or green? I hope green. His eyes are perfect. "You got me pregnant, you asshole! How?!"

And his laugh.

I love his laugh.

Right now I want to choke him because he's laughing. It's still a perfect laugh, though.

"You see," Dr. Venable starts in his doctorly voice that's not so hot at the moment. "Antibiotics lessen the effects of birth control and—"

"You were on three rounds," August reminds me. "We weren't always careful."

Callie will have a sibling. How cool is that?

"What about my career?" I mutter in defeat.

"Like you're the only pregnant woman to be an attorney?" August challenges back.

I'm an attorney. And pregnant. This is the best day of my life.

"Who's pregnant?" Dad asks nosily and then screeches to a halt. "You're…my baby girl…" His throat bobs with emotion.

When all three of us nod at him, he hollers, "My little girl is pregnant!"

A smile tugs at my lips and August winks at me.

"You lost your shit," he says with a smirk.

"I did not lose my shit."

"Oh, here they go," Dad says, chuckling before he kisses the top of my head. "I'm going to make some calls."

Dr. Venable follows him out, leaving us alone.

"You totally did." August's lips find mine.

"Did not."

"It was really hot," he continues. "You know I love when you lose your mind."

"You're an asshole."

"And you're going to be a mommy, Mrs. Miller. What do you have to say for yourself, counselor?"

My bottom lip wobbles. "Thank you."

His brows lift in surprise. "I was expecting a finger."

"I already gave you one," I remind him, wiggling my wedding ring finger at him.

"I love you," he tells me.

"I love you too," I whisper. "I always have."

"You ready to call Callie?"

"She's going to lose her shit."

He laughs. "No one will ever lose their shit like you do, babe."

I shoot him the bird and he shoots me a smile.

All humor fades as the crushing weight of

reality hits me.

"August, I'm scared."

He cradles my cheek and kisses my lips. "I'm not. You're amazing at everything you do. Well, except for cooking. You better let me handle feeding the baby." I shoot him a withering glare that has him chuckling. "But besides that, you're literally the best and smartest at everything. You think you're going to fail at motherhood?" He shakes his head. "I know better."

I expect more teasing, but my big, broody delicious husband climbs into the small bed beside me and holds me as I ponder what being a mother will be like. At first, I feel nervous. But then, the anxiety fades and a familiar determination settles in my bones.

"I've got this," I tell him, confidence bleeding into my words.

He kisses my hair. "I never had any doubt."

The End

If you loved August and Winter in *Red Hot Winter*, you'll love *Bad Bad Bad*!

Bad Bad Bad is free with my newsletter signup and can be found exclusively for purchase on my website.

If you're curious about Lauren from this story… she'll get her own taboo treat soon! You may have met her handsome hero already in *Enzo…*

K WEBSTER'S TABOO WORLD

Cast of Characters

Brandt Smith (Rick's Best Friend)
Kelsey McMahon (Rick's Daughter)
Rick McMahon (Sheriff)
Mandy Halston (Kelsey's Best Friend)

Miles Reynolds (Drew's Best Friend)
Olivia Rowe (Max's Daughter/Sophia's Sister)

Dane Alexander (Max's Best Friend)
Nick Stratton

Judge Maximillian "Max" Rowe (Olivia and
Sophia's Father)
Dorian Dresser

Drew Hamilton (Miles's Best Friend)
Sophia Rowe (Max's Daughter/Olivia's Sister)

Easton McAvoy (Preacher)
Lacy Greenwood (Stephanie's Daughter)

Stephanie Greenwood (Lacy's Mother)
Anthony Blakely (Quinn's Son)
Aiden Blakely (Quinn's Son)

Quinn Blakely (Anthony and Aiden's Father)
Ava Prince (Lacy/Raven/Olivia's friend)

Karelma Bonilla (Mateo's Daughter)
Adam Renner (Principal)

Coach Everett Long (Adam's friend)
River Banks (Olivia's Best Friend)

Mateo Bonilla (Four Fathers Series Side
Character)

Vaughn Young
Vale Young

Enzo Tauber
Jenna Pruitt

August Miller
Winter Burke

K WEBSTER'S TABOO WORLD
READING LIST

These don't necessarily have to be read in order to enjoy, but if you would like to know the order I wrote them in, it is as follows (with more being added to as I publish):

Bad Bad Bad
Coach Long
Ex-Rated Attraction
Mr. Blakely
Malfeasance
Easton (Formerly known as Preach)
Crybaby
Lawn Boys
Renner's Rules
The Glue
Dane
Enzo
Red Hot Winter

BOOKS BY
K WEBSTER

Psychological Romance Standalones:

My Torin

Whispers and the Roars

Cold Cole Heart

Blue Hill Blood

Romantic Suspense Standalones:

Dirty Ugly Toy

El Malo

Notice

Sweet Jayne

The Road Back to Us

Surviving Harley

Love and Law

Moth to a Flame

Erased

Extremely Forbidden Romance Standalones:

The Wild

Hale

Taboo Treats:
Bad Bad Bad
Coach Long
Ex-Rated Attraction
Mr. Blakely
Easton
Crybaby
Lawn Boys
Malfeasance
Renner's Rules
The Glue
Dane
Enzo
Red Hot Winter

Contemporary Romance Standalones:
The Day She Cried
Untimely You
Heath
Sundays are for Hangovers
A Merry Christmas with Judy
Zeke's Eden
Schooled by a Senior
Give Me Yesterday
Sunshine and the Stalker
Bidding for Keeps
B-Sides and Rarities

Paranormal Romance Standalones:
Apartment 2B
Running Free
Mad Sea

War & Peace Series:
This is War, Baby (Book 1)
This is Love, Baby (Book 2)
This Isn't Over, Baby (Book 3)
This Isn't You, Baby (Book 4)
This is Me, Baby (Book 5)
This Isn't Fair, Baby (Book 6)
This is the End, Baby (Book 7—a novella)

Lost Planet Series:
The Forgotten Commander (Book 1)

2 Lovers Series:
Text 2 Lovers (Book 1)
Hate 2 Lovers (Book 2)
Thieves 2 Lovers (Book 3)

Pretty Little Dolls Series:
Pretty Stolen Dolls (Book 1)
Pretty Lost Dolls (Book 2)
Pretty New Doll (Book 3)
Pretty Broken Dolls (Book 4)

The V Games Series:
Vlad (Book 1)
Ven (Book 2)
Vas (Book 3)

Four Fathers Books:
Pearson

Four Sons Books:
Camden

Not Safe for Amazon Books:
The Wild
Hale
Bad Bad Bad
This is War, Baby

The Breaking the Rules Series:
Broken (Book 1)
Wrong (Book 2)
Scarred (Book 3)
Mistake (Book 4)
Crushed (Book 5—a novella)

The Vegas Aces Series:
Rock Country (Book 1)
Rock Heart (Book 2)
Rock Bottom (Book 3)

The Becoming Her Series:
Becoming Lady Thomas (Book 1)
Becoming Countess Dumont (Book 2)
Becoming Mrs. Benedict (Book 3)

Alpha & Omega Duet:
Alpha & Omega (Book 1)
Omega & Love (Book 2)

ACKNOWLEDGEMENTS

Thank you to my husband. You're always my inspiration! I love you bunches!

I want to give a huge shout out of thanks to the ladies of Read Me Romance—Alexa Riley and Tessa Bailey, thank you for including me in on your fun podcast and encouraging me to write this story!

A huge thank you to my Krazy for K Webster's Books reader group. You all are insanely supportive and I can't thank you enough.

A gigantic thank you to those who always help me out. Elizabeth Clinton, Ella Stewart, Misty Walker, Holly Sparks, Jillian Ruize, Gina Behrends, Jessica Hollyfield, Ker Dukey, and Nikki Ash—you ladies are my rock!

Thank you so much to Misty for loving my stories and encouraging me every step of the way! You're an awesome friend and I'm so thankful to have you in my life! When I need someone to use SHOUTY CAPS ABOUT HOW AWESOME MY ACHIEVEMENTS ARE, I can always count on you. I love you more than you'll ever know!

A huge shoutout of thanks to Jillian Ruize for uncovering a big uh-oh in the story that needed some last minute reconstructive surgery...my perfectionist brain thanks you a million times over!!

A big thank you to my author friends who have given me your friendship and your support. You have no idea how much that means to me.

Thank you to all of my blogger friends both big and small that go above and beyond to always share my stuff. You all rock! #AllBlogsMatter

Emily A. Lawrence, thank you SO much for editing this book. You're amazing and I can't thank you enough! Love you!

Thank you Stacey Blake for being amazing as always when formatting my books and in general. I love you! I love you! I love you!

A big thanks to my PR gal, Nicole Blanchard. You are fabulous at what you do and keep me on track!

Lastly but certainly not least of all, thank you to all of the wonderful readers out there who are willing to hear my story and enjoy my characters like I do. It means the world to me!

ABOUT THE AUTHOR

K Webster is the *USA Today* bestselling author of over seventy romance books in many different genres including contemporary romance, historical romance, paranormal romance, dark romance, romantic suspense, taboo romance, and erotic romance. When not spending time with her hilarious and handsome husband and two adorable children, she's active on social media connecting with her readers.

Her other passions besides writing include reading and graphic design. K can always be found in front of her computer chasing her next idea and taking action. She looks forward to the day when she will see one of her titles on the big screen.

Join K Webster's newsletter to receive a couple of updates a month on new releases and exclusive content. To join, all you need to do is go here (www.authorkwebster.com).

Facebook:

www.facebook.com/authorkwebster

Blog:

authorkwebster.wordpress.com

Twitter:

twitter.com/KristiWebster

Email:

kristi@authorkwebster.com

Goodreads:

www.goodreads.com/user/show/10439773-k-
webster

Instagram:

instagram.com/kristiwebster

K WEBSTER'S

Taboo World

two interconnected stories

BAD
BAD
BAD

two taboo treats

k webster

Bad Bad Bad

Two interconnected stories. Two taboo treats.

Brandt's Cherry Girl

He's old enough to be her father.
She's his best friend's daughter.
Their connection is off the charts.
And so very, very wrong.
This can't happen.
Oh, but it already is…

Sheriff's Bad Girl

He's the law and follows the rules.
She's wild and out of control.
His daughter's best friend is trouble.
And he wants to punish her…
With his teeth.

USA TODAY BESTSELLING AUTHOR
K WEBSTER
She's a hurdle in his way...
and he wants to jump her.
a taboo treat
COACH
LONG

Coach Long

Coach Everett Long has a chip on his shoulder.
Working every day with the man who stole his
fiancée leaves him pissed and on edge.
His temper is volatile and his attitude sucks.

River Banks is a funky-styled runner
with a bizarre past.
Starting over at a new school was supposed to
be easy…but she should have known better.
She likes to antagonize and tends to go after
what she's not supposed to have.

When the arrogant bully meets the strong-willed
brat, it sparks an illicit attraction.
Together, they heat up the track with
longing and desire.
Everything about their chemistry is wrong.
So why does it feel so right?

She's a hurdle in his way and, dear God does
he want to jump her.
Will she be worth the risk or
will he fall flat on his face?

Ex-Rated Attraction

I liked Caleb.

I like his dad more.

Miles Reynolds sent shocks through me the very first time I met him. With his full beard and sculpted ass, he's every inch a heroic, powerful Greek god.

He saved me from a bad situation and now he's all I can think of. Every minute of every hour of every day, I want that man.

He's warned me away, says I can't handle what he has to give.

But I know better.

Miles is exactly what I need—now, then and forever.

Mr. Blakely

It started as a job.

It turned into so much more.

Mr. Blakely is strict with his sons, but he's soft and gentle with me.

The powerful businessman is something else entirely when we're together.

Boss, teacher, lover…husband.

My hopes and dreams for the future have changed. I want—no, I need—him by my side.

a taboo treat

malfeasance

Judge Rowe
never had
a problem with
morality...
until her.

USA TODAY BESTSELLING AUTHOR
K WEBSTER

Malfeasance

Max Rowe always follows the rules.
A successful judge.
A single father.
A leader in the community.
Doing the right thing means everything.

But when he finds himself rescuing an incredibly
young woman,
everything he's worked hard for is quickly
forgotten.
The only thing that matters is keeping her safe.
She's gorgeous, intelligent, and the ultimate
temptation.
Doing the wrong thing suddenly feels right.

Their chemistry is intense.
It's a romance no one will approve of, yet one they
can't ignore.
Hot, fast, and explosive.
Someone is going to get burned.

He'll give up everything for her…
because without her, he is nothing.

EASTON

K WEBSTER

Easton

A man who made countless mistakes.
A woman with a messy past.

He's tasked with helping her find her way.
She's lost in grief and self-doubt.

Together they begin something innocent…
Until it's not.

His freedom is at risk.
Her heart won't survive another break.

All rational thinking says they
should stay away from each other.
But neither are very good
at following the rules.

A deep, dark craving.
An overwhelming need.
A burn much hotter than any hell
they could ever be condemned to.

He'll give up everything for her…
because without her, he is nothing.

He likes her screams.
He likes them an awful lot.

Crybaby

a taboo treat

K WEBSTER

Crybaby

Stubborn.

Mouthy.

Brazen.

Two people with vicious tongues.

A desperate temptation neither can ignore.

An injury has changed her entire life.

She's crippled, hopeless, and angry.

And the only one who can lessen her pain is him.

Being the boss is sometimes a pain in the ass.

He's irritated, impatient, and doesn't play games.

Yet he's the only one willing to fight her…for her.

Daring.

Forbidden.

Out of control.

Someone is going to get hurt.

And, oh, how painfully sweet that will be.

The grass is greener where
he points his hose...

lawn
BOYS
a taboo treat

USA TODAY BESTSELLING AUTHOR
K WEBSTER

Lawn Boys

She's lived her life and it has been a good one.
Marriage. College. A family.
Slowly, though, life moved forward and left her at
a standstill.

Until the lawn boy barges into her world.
Bossy. Big. Sexy as hell.
A virile young male to remind her she's all woman.

Too bad she's twice his age.
Too bad he doesn't care.

She's older and wiser and more mature.
Which means absolutely nothing when he's
invading her space.

K WEBSTER

Principal Renner,
I've been *bad*.
Again.

a taboo treat

RENNER'S
Rules

Renner's Rules

I'm a bad girl.

I was sent away.

New house. New rules. New school.

Change was supposed to be…good.

Until I met him.

No one warned me Principal Renner would be so hot.

I'd expected some old, graying man in a brown suit.

Not this.

Not well over six feet of lean muscle and piercing green eyes.

Not a rugged-faced, ax-wielding lumberjack of a man.

He's grouchy and rude and likes to boss me around.

I find myself getting in trouble just so he'll punish me.

Especially with his favorite metal ruler.

Being bad never felt so good

USA TODAY BESTSELLING AUTHOR
K WEBSTER
Two people.
Their unraveling
marriage.
And they want
me to be...
the
GLUE
a taboo treat

The Glue

I'm a fixer. A lover. Always searching for the right
fit.
And I come up empty every time.
My desires are unusual.
I don't feel whole until I'm in the middle, holding
it all together.
Which makes having a romantic relationship
really difficult.

Until them.
Two people. An unraveling marriage. Love on the
rocks.
And they want me.
To put them back together again.

Problem is, once they're fixed, where does that
leave me?
I sure as hell hope I stick like glue.

USA TODAY BESTSELLING AUTHOR
K WEBSTER
He was the boss in
the bedroom.
I was the boss outside of it.
Two alphas.
One hot agenda.
DANE
a taboo treat

I'm used to being in charge.
In the courtroom. In life. In the bedroom.
But then I met him.

He brings me *literally* to my knees.

Handsome. Charismatic. Sexy as hell.
He's everything I desperately crave to possess.

I'm burning to get him beneath me just to have a
taste.
Turns out, though, one taste isn't enough.
And he's starved for me too.

Two alphas fighting for dominance.
He thrives on control and I can't give it up.

A battle of wills.
The bedroom is the battlefield and our hearts are
on the line.

USA TODAY BESTSELLING AUTHOR
K WEBSTER
SHE DOESN'T NEED A HERO. SHE JUST NEEDS HIM.
en
A TABOO TREAT
zo

Jenna's grown up in the system.
Forced to be tough, wary, and hard.

She's only been able to count on herself.
Until Enzo.
He's much older and responsible for looking after her.
What should be a job to him, evolves into much more.

Late night phone calls.
Lingering touches.
A forbidden fire that burns brighter each day.

Everything about him exudes strength.
His will to protect her is more than she could ever ask for.
Sadly, though, even heroes have their limitations.

But she doesn't need a hero.
She just needs him.

52078601R00111

Made in the USA
Columbia, SC
02 March 2019